A December to Remember

Sarah Mitches

Contents

1. Chapter 1   1
2. Chapter 2   5
3. Chapter 3   9
4. Chapter 4   13
5. Chapter 5   17
6. Chapter 6   23
7. Chapter 7   27
8. Chapter 8   33
9. Chapter 9   39
10. Chapter 10   46
11. Chapter 11   50
12. Chapter 12   56
13. Chapter 13   61
14. Chapter 14   65
15. Chapter 15   74
16. Chapter 16   78
17. Chapter 17   85

18. Chapter 18   88

19. Chapter 19   93

20. Chapter 20   97

21. Chapter 21   103

22. Chapter 22   110

23. Chapter 23   116

24. Chapter 24   124

25. Chapter 25   127

26. Chapter 26   134

27. Chapter 27   138

28. Chapter 28   142

29. Chapter 29   145

30. Chapter 30   150

31. Epilogue   156

Chapter 1

The first time I saw you, it was a Saturday. December first. I don't know if you remember it, because you have so many words in your head that sometimes the little things slip out, but I do.

I remember because I was sitting alone in that little teashop on 23rd street, the one where all the college kids come in scarves and sweaters when it's cold. There was a candle on my table in a little glass cup, and it smelled like peppermint. Or maybe that was my tea.

When you came in, I had my head buried in book whose name I can no longer remember. I've read too many, I guess. I didn't look up; people are always coming into the tea house, coming and leaving and coming back again because the tea here is the best in all of Portland. That's what Krystal says, anyway, and she's the owner so I guess she would know. Krystal also says that I'm here so much, I practically blend into the scenery, and one day someone will come in and sit on me because they'll think that I'm a chair. That kind of hurts, if I'm honest, but I don't say so. Krystal doesn't get things like that.

But you didn't blend in with the scenery, not at all. I wasn't paying attention at first, and all I heard was the faint murmur of your voice ordering a drink ('Vanilla bubble tea, please. Yes, warm sounds nice. No, I'll pass on the tapioca.'). Even that came through a haze, because you know I have a knack for blocking things out when I'm reading. You slipped away from the counter after ordering, and I only know that because a moment later, you appeared in the seating area in a flash of bright goldenrod.

That drew my attention: you were wearing a garish raincoat the same color as the flame of the candle on my table. It clashed terribly with the dark wood of the cafe, but somehow you managed to pull it off. With your auburn hair hanging damp down your back and the polka-dotted umbrella dangling from your wrist, you looked like an awkward girl out of one of those movies that my aunt loves to watch. The rom-coms, I think?

And maybe you collected a few odd stares, because we were all regulars and you were a newbie, but I was captivated by you. Not many things can pull me from a book, you know. But you did, and that made me watch you, discreetly, as you scouted for a seat.

There was an empty chair across from me, but I didn't speak up because I'd probably end up looking stupid and besides, did I really want company? Anyway, you found a place to sit soon enough, on the corner of the couch next to that bookshelf full of boardgames. You prodded the guy who had his stuff on the cushion there, and he grunted and shifted his bag to the floor, all without looking at you. You didn't seem to mind.

There were headphones over your ears (I could hear the music from my table five feet away; it was Norah Jones), and I guess that's why you didn't realize how much noise you were making. The bag over your shoulder had a really loud zipper, and the sound of it sliced, knife-like, through the soft music wandering about the cafe.

You pulled out a laptop, set it on the couch, then thought better of it and picked it up again. It was small; a netbook ensconced in a purple case.

Some people gave you dirty looks as you bumbled around, working your way out of that heinous coat and tossing it unceremoniously onto the ground. You had a sweater on beneath it, a thick red one with a polar bear's face on the front, and gloves tucked into the sleeves. It looked warm. Your rain boots squeaked on the hardwood floor as you settled into place with the netbook in your lap, not noticing when the guy beside you scooted a little bit farther away.

All of your things were scattered, crushed beneath you or slung across your legs, so that it looked like getting up would be near impossible. Maybe that's why you groaned when the barista called your order (I don't know how you heard her, your music was so loud), and you had to untangle yourself in order to stand. That guy got up and found a new seat while you were gone.

You came back quickly, a blue mug of tea wafting steam into your eyes. Your image becoming distorted as you passed before the little candlelight flame, but I could still see the smirk on your lips. There was a rosy, wind-kissed blush to your cheeks, but I didn't think you looked cold. Just happy, smiling at a private joke inside your mind. Later, I'd be privy to those amusements, but at the moment, I was just watching, quietly.

My head was partly shielded by my book, leaving only my eyes were visible, like a proper stalker. And when you set your drink down and turned around, your gaze sweeping over me, I quickly slapped my book down reverted my focus to the pages in front of me. The movement upset the flame, making it stutter and dance.

You didn't even notice me staring (you had that blank look in your eyes), but I didn't want to take the chance. I'd never seen you before, and I didn't want you to be scared away from the teashop by that one weird boy who had a particular fondness for people-watching.

So I made myself read for the rest of the next two hours, even though I finished the book and ended up starting again from the beginning. I heard you typing, though, your fingers making that rapid, lovely sound of nails against computer keys. What were you writing? I wondered. But of course I didn't ask, because then I'd just look like a fool. And why did I care, anyway? I'd never seen you before in my life; you were just another pretty girl who happened to find her way into the teashop.

But in the back of my mind, I had to admit that I found you fascinating. You were so oblivious to everything around you, but you focused on that computer screen as if it was your salvation. And it was, I guess. I know that now.

You left at four PM, without warning, and it seemed as if you were rushing. As you sped past my table, the stray flapping sleeve of your jacket snuffed out my candle. You didn't notice. I didn't mind.

Chapter 2

Sunday was December second, and it was also the day that my Aunt Sheridan decided to start our Christmas shopping. She had received a Macy's catalogue in the mail, and when I came down for breakfast, she was standing at the kitchen counter in a pink bathrobe, her hair in curlers, sifting through it avidly. Uncle Dillon was perched on a stool at the kitchen table, coffee mug in one hand and newspaper in the other, and neither of them looked up as I clomped down the stairs.

As per usual.

"Dill," Aunt Sheridan cooed, flipping the magazine around to face her husband, "look at this coffeemaker! It's fifty percent off today, should I buy it?"

I was at the fridge, but I heard Uncle Dillon's groan. I could see it in my head: he had put down his paper, and now he was squeezing the bridge of his nose between two weathered fingers, his head shaking slowly back and forth. I knew this because it happened every morning, since Aunt Sheridan is a full-time bargain hunter who sees fit to buy anything if it's at a discounted price.

"Sheridan," said my uncle, sternly. "We do not need another coffeemaker. We have, what, six already?"

"Seven," I mumbled, my eyes flicking to the cabinet where they're stored.

"Oh." Aunt Sheridan's voice drooped. But when I turned from the fridge, a package of frozen waffles in hand, she smiled at me. You know that smile, she gives it to you all the time. It's the one that you see and think, oh shit, I am screwed.

"Sam, I was thinking of doing some Christmas shopping at the mall today. Do you want to come?"

No, Aunt Sheridan, I do not want to go to the mall, because I might see people I know and they'll laugh and laugh at me for being with my aunt in public.

"Sure, Aunt Sheridan," I piped, forcing a smile onto my lips. Because I knew it was hard for her sometimes, being the only female creature in the house since my sister moved out. And if I really did see someone from school, there were plenty of clothing racks to hide in.

The mall was hopelessly crowded, but that didn't stop Aunt Sheridan from powering through the masses the way you do when you're trying to get to the food table at your family parties. It was nice, though, because there was Christmas music playing and wreaths and lights hung everywhere and a giant tree at the center of the food court.

I hoped to avoid attracting attention, but that's impossible when my aunt enjoys wearing neon green track suits that are about two sizes too small for her plump stature. And I did see people from school, because of course this is where they all hang out, all the time. I tried to stay out of the way, but I think Carson Myles on the football team saw me, because he was pointing and laughing with all he buddies.

I ducked behind a mannequin so I wouldn't have to see.

We only went to Macy's, because Aunt Sheridan had that catalogue and she was very eager to use it. You hate that store, but I didn't know that then.

"Sam," Aunt Sheridan called, perusing through the girl's section, "what should we get for Brianna?"

Brianna was my cousin in Montana, the bratty fourteen-year-old who rides horses and hates everyone in the family. We should get her coal, is what I was thinking.

I couldn't respond though, because I suddenly heard a sharp whistle, and the sound of a familiar voice calling my name. "Yo, Windermere!" It was Carson Myles, of course, because I have such damn bad luck that it really couldn't be anyone else. I froze, my hand on the sleeve of a glittering pink sweater.. Don't turn around don't turn around don't you dare turn around—

I turned around. Idiot.

Carson was standing there with his arm around one of those girls you hate, the slutty kind who show off their butts even when it's forty degrees outside, and his usual posse of guys was flanking him. He had this big, ugly grin on his face, and his girlfriend-thing was laughing daintily behind her hand.

"So I guess it's true, eh?" he quipped. "Sammy Windermere does wear girl's clothes!"

And then they were all laughing, laughing at me, and I was reeling back, back, back behind the sweater display, thinking please don't follow me, please.

They didn't follow, but I felt the redness of my face, the hurt in my stomach, the burning behind my eyes. Pathetic.

"Sa-mu-el!" shouted my aunt, in her loud, loud, too loud voice. "Come here!"

I still heard them laughing, but maybe it was in my head, so I stumbled after my aunt's voice, swiping violently at my eyes. She was by the coats, examining several different styles with her beady brown eyes. That catalogue was still clutched between her red nails.

"Which one do you think she'd like better? Black, or brown?"

I glanced over the coats, but they looked the same to me. I don't know why girls make shopping such a big deal, or why it mattered whether a coat was brown or black or hell, periwinkle. And I certainly didn't understand why people got picked on for doing nothing but helping their aunt do her Christmas shopping.

"Sam," Aunt Sheridan snapped. "Which one?"

I scanned the coats again, and was just about to give an answer when my eyes caught on something over my aunt's left shoulder. It was a raincoat. A bright, terrible yellow raincoat that made me think of you.

"What about that one?" I pointed.

Aunt Sheridan turned. "Of course not that one, that's hideous! You know that Bree hates yellow!"

No, Aunt Sheridan, I don't know that. And I don't see how your limey-puke sweatpants are any better than this.

I shoved my hands into my jean pockets, shrugging. "Whoops, forgot. Brown, I guess. I don't know what I was thinking."

I didn't know what I was thinking.

I guess I was thinking about you.

Chapter 3

I think that Monday is my favorite day of the week, because on Mondays, my aunt and uncle are at work and can't pick me up from school. Walking home isn't so great, of course, especially during a rainy spell, but I can tolerate it because if I go a little bit out of my way, I pass by the amazing bookstore on Burnside, the one that stretches for an entire city block and has every book ever written in the history of mankind.

Except that by 'pass by', I basically mean go inside and spend hours among the shelves.

I always tell myself, no, Sam, not today; you're going to go straight home, and that's that. But maybe I'm not so good at self-control, because my feet always end up walking through the front door even as my brain is insisting that we continue on. I always lose to myself, anyway, but I guess I just like to pretend that one week I won't.

I gave in again that Monday, and as I went inside I thought that it's lucky I'm not a drug addict, because I'd never be able to stop giving in. You told me once that maybe books are my drug, and I think that's okay. At the very least, it's better than the shit those kids are always smoking in the bathrooms before school, when they think nobody is watching.

It was warm in the bookstore; it's always warm in the bookstore. Everyone was smiling, laughing, reading, because let's be honest with ourselves: it's impossible not to be happy when you have a book in your hands.

I have a tendency to wander through the aisles, not even looking, just breathing, running my fingers over the spines of the volumes and watching people's secret smiles as they uncovered a novel they'd been searching for forever. That's what I was doing when I somehow found my way into the little cafe that caps off the end of the store, where they brew the best Peruvian coffee in all of Portland, and saw someone who was startlingly familiar.

You.

My immediate reaction was to leap behind a shelf, which, in hindsight, was pretty stupid. If you had been looking, I would have just drawn more attention to myself. But you weren't; you were sitting by yourself at one of the round tables with a book and notebook under each elbow, respectively, a pen in your hand, and a paper cup of coffee resting beneath your chin. As I poked my head around a case of self-help books, I saw that you were also wearing a tie-dyed neon t-shirt that was way too big, the kind of thing that would make Aunt Sheridan gag. You later told me that your younger brother made it for you in camp one year, but at the time I just thought that you had terrible fashion sense.

I liked the shirt, though.

Your hair was in a bun that had come loose, and it hung into your face so that every few seconds, you had to pause to blow your bangs away. From the look on your face, it was annoying you, but you were so glued to that notebook in front of you that you refused to pause in your writing to fix it.

You were writing. Again. I wondered for a second time what you were writing; were you a poet? A diarist? J.K. Rowling in disguise? Possibly. But regardless, I found myself enthralled as I watched you, the way every ounce of your energy was focused on that one page. I didn't understand how words could be so important to a person, but I guess they are for you.

I don't know how long I stood there, crouched behind the shelves in a completely obvious way, but it was long enough for the man behind the counter of the cafe to start eyeing me funny. My face in flames, I sneaked out awkwardly and made my way over to the magnetic poetry easel over by the Victorian fiction display. I'm shit with poems, but I rearranged the words absently and just kept watching you out of the corner of my eye.

You took a sip of your coffee (was it java? Colombian? Sumatran?), and when you set the cup back down, I saw the letters of your name scrawled in messy script across the side. E-L-L-E-R-Y. Ellery. Ellery. I murmured the syllables to myself. Ellery.

You looked up suddenly. I whirled around quickly. You slowly went back to your writing, and I breathed out a sigh of relief. I had to stop this; there's nothing healthy about a fascination with a girl who you've never spoken to. Either I would go talk to you, or I would leave.

Maybe, if I were a bolder person, I would have strode right over to your table and sat down at the empty seat, said, Hey Ellery, I'm Sam, and you're beautiful. And you would have smiled the way girls do in movies, and I would have been cool for once in my life.

I'm not a bold person, though, and you weren't the kind of girl who'd look twice at me anyway. So I just left, left you there in your tie-dyed shirt, writing, and walked home in the rain feeling like the world's biggest wimp.

Chapter 4

I have three neighbors: the people in apartment on the left, the people in the apartment on the right, and the people in the apartment across the hall. I guess if you're looking at the big picture, I actually have somewhere around thirty neighbors, because that's about how many apartments are on the fourth floor. But I only count those three, because I see them everyday and sometimes they actually acknowledge my existence.

To the left is Mr. Marion, an old man with a stoop whose wife died of cancer ten years ago. He's reserved and gruff, and he's also the postman for our neighborhood. It's weird to think that postmen have homes and hopes and cares and lives, because I always just thought that they climbed into a mailbox at night and curled up among the unsent letters.

To the right is the Lainey residence: a mom, a dad, and a girl named Margeaux. Margeaux is a year older than us, so she's graduated, but she still lives at home because she's going to photography school in the city. She's very pretty in a dramatic way, since she's mixed with about fifty different races and that makes her look like an exotic princess. I used to have a really big crush on her, and she would smile at me whenever we crossed on the way to our apartments, but then my sister told me something very terrible about Margeaux's reputation and now I just see her and feel kind of sad.

But it's my neighbors across the hall that are most important: Mr. and Mrs. Reagan. They're a really young couple, and they're true hippies; they both wear their hair long and have peace tattoos and talk about their protest movements on the way down the elevator. They are nice, though, if a little weird, and they're very much in love. You can tell because they're always smiling at each other, laughing together, and they constantly looked like they're in this special little world that only they know.

On Wednesday the fourth of December, my aunt dropped me off at the apartment building after school, while she went to get groceries. I took the stairs up, because Carson and his friends had been particularly brutal that day and constant movement helped me to stop thinking about it. Mr. and Mrs. Reagan (or Martin and Suzy, as they insist I call them) were taking the stairs too, except they were above me and I was so busy being bothered that I didn't see them there, paused on the third floor landing as they organized the bags in their arms.

Honestly, I think I might be the only person in the world who can be more clumsy than you; I crashed right into the pair of them. There was a crash and a shriek, and when I turned there were garlands and lights and wrapping paper all strewn across the floor, the product of an afternoon of decoration shopping and one awkward boy who just always has to wreck things for everyone.

"I'm so sorry," I mumbled, hooking my thumbs nervously into the straps of my backpack. But Martin and Suzy just smiled, and told me that it's okay because I just added some spice to their afternoon and thank you for that.

They're odd people. I was just glad they weren't mad.

I hurried up the stairs again after my offer to help them clean up was denied, because I didn't want to cause even more trouble. But I paused before rounding the corner and glanced over my shoulder to make sure the Reagans were okay.

They were better than okay, I'd say. They were smiling at each other—smiling, smiling, always smiling—and Martin looped a garland around Suzy's shoulders to pull her close, close, closer. Her arms snaked around his neck, and she was looking at him like he was the best thing that ever happened to her, and he was grinning down at her like she was absolutely perfect.

I turned around when they kissed, because kisses are private things for two happy people and not bumbling guys named Sam. But as I trudged up to my apartment, I was thinking, I couldn't stop thinking: I want someone to smile at me like that. I want to have someone whom I can smile at like that.

And then your face, inexplicably, flashed into my mind. Or maybe it was explicable, because I'd been seeing it in there a lot lately. I saw you smiling at me, a smile that I'd never really seen but could imagine forming so easily on your lips—

At the door to my apartment, I decided: I was going to talk to you. The next time I saw you, there would be no excuses. I wasn't going to blow it again, because maybe I'd run out of chances after that, and then where would I be?

And if things worked out like the stupid, fantastical little dream in my head, we'd end up like Suzy and Martin one day. But we wouldn't have the tattoos and the picket signs and most definitely not the long hair, because you're the only one of us who could actually pull it off.

I'd have to actually talk to you first, though, and that was a step. A leap, actually. But I was determined and convinced and for once, confident. I was going to do this.

No excuses.

Chapter 5

The couches in the teashop are patched and sagging. They bend under human weight, creaking and groaning in their low, protesting voices whenever anyone dares to take a seat. Krystal says that they're "vintage" and therefore add to the atmosphere of the place, but I think she's just too cheap to buy new ones.

They're comfortable enough, anyway, and I suppose they're perfect for drinking tea and reading quietly when it's cold outside. And it was very cold on Wednesday, so of course, I had my aunt leave me at the teashop after school.

It smelled like tea inside: leafy and herbal and sweet and calming, and the scent washed over me and suddenly everything was okay. Like puzzle pieces into place, click, click, click. And after I'd ordered my drink and had a steaming mug in my hands, I decided that there was just something oddly aligning about hot tea on cold days. The two just fit together, like peanut butter and jelly, like Martin and Suzy, like Christmas and twinkling lights.

Maybe one day, I thought, like you and me.

The only open place was a dinky old loveseat which Krystal swears once belonged Joan Plantagenet, daughter of King Edward III. Maybe that makes sense, because that was centuries ago and that little couch sure is rickety. Everyone tends to steer clear of it like it has the plague.

Irony's a funny thing, you know; Joan Plantagenet was killed by the plague.

Uncertainty made me sit down gingerly, carefully, half-convinced that any sudden movements would snap the seat in two. It was a balancing act, because I had a book in one hand and a teacup in the other and I'm not exactly what you'd call a coordinated individual. I managed, though, and the springs sighed beneath me like a breathy murmur of relief.

The teashop was quiet, but it wasn't that kind of pensive silence that means pressed lips and withheld breath. No, this sort of silence was gentle and wispy; it was clouds on sky and brushes on canvas. It was fragile, like sugar glass. And it was the only thing I heard when the bell jingled, and the door opened, and you came shivering inside.

I was rereading The Hobbit, because the movie was due out soon, but I forgot about it in a second when I happened to glance up and you were approaching the counter. You passed by the teacup display along the wall, your hair glistening with a million beads of rain that couldn't stand to let you go.

For a few brief moments, you slipped from my view as you ordered your drink. Play it cool, Sam, I thought to myself. Not a big deal. I tried to focus back on my reading, but that didn't really work out until you came back around, mug in hand, and I had to drill my gaze down so it wouldn't seem like I'd been looking at you.

I lifted an eye, discreetly, to watch as you scanned the room for an empty seat, then arched back onto your toes and checked the other room over your shoulder. You kneaded your bottom lip with your teeth, your eyes cloudy. Unsure. You were unsure, and maybe it was wrong, but that reassured me because I was unsure a lot too.

For instance, I was unsure in my head at that moment, as you shifted awkwardly and let your messenger bag bounce against your knees. On one hand, I wanted to call out to you, ask if you wanted the seat beside me even though it was small and shaky. But on the other hand, that familiar tension was building in my gut, and I kind of just wanted to curl up into a ball, too.

Come on, Sam, you've got to be kidding me, snapped that critical little voice in my head. No excuses.

I swallowed. I scratched at the sleeve of my sweater. I let out a quiet cough, so quiet that maybe I was hoping you wouldn't hear it.

But you did, and you turned slightly as I looked back to my book once again. Perhaps, if I had been more confident, I would have smiled at you and beckoned you over and we would have hit it off right away. Perhaps, if I stopped if-ing all the time, I wouldn't be so down on myself. You're always pestering me about that, after all.

You walked over: I watched your boots shuffle toward me, a pair of sweatpants tucked into them sloppily. When you stopped in front of me, I allowed myself to look up to you. Our eyes met-yours were green.

"Excuse me," you murmured, "can I sit here?"

Your voice: it was both soft and scratchy at once, like that reindeer sweater your grandmother made for you this Christmas. Your words blended together, effortlessly, in this lovely stream of lingual prosody that was even more soothing than silence. You were careful and bright and pretty, and I was so busy staring that I very nearly forgot to answer your question.

"Oh-um-of course!"

You thanked me, a hint of a smirk playing on your lips, and sat down beside me. The stupid loveseat wailed, and your hand flew to your lips as a few people glanced our way.

"It's okay," I assured quickly, "this piece of junk is ancient."

A blush had crept onto your neck, but you nodded.

After that, you pulled out your netbook and I pretended not to watch you, and it was quiet once again save for the soft clink of your nails against your cerulean mug. And then, soon after, the tap of your fingers on computer keys.

I really was reading now, promise, but I'd glance over every few seconds. I'd see you there, completely enthralled by whatever you were typing on that screen. It was as if I was watching a kid in a candy store: your eyes were wide. And of course, I wondered what was so fantastic about a glowing little screen.

Several times, I almost asked. I wanted to ask. But asking meant words, and words meant vulnerability. I used to think that's what they meant, anyway. You've since taught me differently.

Sam, if you want to know, just open your mouth and ask her. She's a girl, not a dinosaur.

I knew you weren't a dinosaur (you were much prettier than a dinosaur), but I think I'd be less afraid to speak if you were. Girls weren't exactly my area of expertise, to say the least. In fact, I was basically certain that I repelled them.

Debating, debating. War inside my mind, wondering: should I, or should I not? It was far too much energy spent on such a simple decision. I guess indecision is just my specialty.

At one point, when I glanced over, you were laughing. I felt myself flush, automatically thinking that you were laughing at me, but your eyes were still glued to the screen. Your fingers flew across the keys, and there was this smile on your lips-it stretched across your face, and it was so utterly pleased and content that I found myself immediately jealous of whatever had caused it.

I wondered if you'd hidden another world inside that little laptop, because it sure seemed like it. As you typed, it was if you'd exited reality and transcended to somewhere else, somewhere better. Somewhere like heaven, but made of hand-typed words.

I had to know. But should I ask? What if I sounded stupid, or imposing, or I tripped over my words and you thought I was an idiot, or what if questions were an insult in your culture and I secured myself a permanent place on your hate list-

"What are you typing?"

Four words, quick and easy. Maybe too quick, but that was okay. I worry too much sometimes.

You looked up abruptly, your eyes like a deer caught in head-lights, your lips in a little O.

"O-oh," you murmured, scratching at your neck. "It's, um, it's a book. A story. I-ah-write stories sometimes."

Talking about it made you nervous, I could tell. But there was a proud flush to your cheeks, and I knew somehow that you were glad I asked. And I thought it was cool, that you were a writer. Maybe I didn't understand it then, because I knew that words were important but I didn't realize what they meant to you, but I thought it was cool.

I told you that, and your lips twitched like you wanted to give me a better adjective. But you just thanked me. You sounded more sure of yourself. You sounded happy. I remembered your private smiles and I wondered if you really were-happy, I mean. I hoped so.

Neither of us spoke again after that, not until Aunt Sheridan called to say that she was waiting outside. That's when I stood and picked up my book and empty mug, and you looked up at me and chirped a peppy, "Goodbye!"

I smiled, feeling oddly light. "Goodbye," I replied. Ellery. But I didn't say your name, because that would sound creepy and I didn't want that. You were looking at your computer again anyway, crawling deeper and deeper into that web of words that fit, that clicked together. Like cold days and hot tea. I glanced back one more time: you were captivated by the screen. I was captivated by you. You, and the way that fictional worlds were woven into reality beneath your fingertips.

Chapter 6

I have favorites. I have a lot of favorites, actually. There's my favorite color (gray), and my favorite animal (capybara), and my favorite movie (The Birds). There are plenty of other things too, but none of them really matter to anyone but me.

My favorite day of the week, though—that's a big deal, because it's Thursday. I guess that by saying "because," I'm kind of making it sound like everyone should know why Thursday is such a great day. And I might be the only person in my entire school who really cares, but Thursday is the day that the weekly meeting of the Lincoln High book club commences. Sure, there are only five of us, but that's more than the one it used to be when it was just me, reading alone in the school library.

They say that misery loves company, and I guess it's true. Maybe I'm not a people person, but I do like the meetings, even though the other club members are indifferent at best. Well, except for Carolina Knowles.

Her last name has the word "know" in it, and it actually fits quite perfectly because she's the biggest know-it-all I have ever met. I already know that you would hate her, because on top of that, it was forty degrees outside and her shirt barely skimmed her midriff. But Carolina was the unofficial club president, a role that I would have taken except that I'm too shy, and nobody else cared enough to object when she decided that she was in charge. Unofficially.

She called that Thursday's meeting to order in her usual way, which was by banging two books together in a way that made me wince. Her lips were pursed, and she was looking down her long nose at us, condescending as ever.

"Today," she sneered, "we were supposed to have read the next five chapters of Anthem. Is everyone caught up?"

I was more than caught up. I'd finished Anthem in one night, then gone on to the next book on our list, then the next one. I couldn't help it; they were addicting. But when I told Carolina that, she just wrinkled her nose like she smelled something bad.

"Sam," she said. Sam, like my name was a disappointing movie or a terrible disease. "Sam, don't you think you're being kind of, I don't know, inconsiderate to the rest of us? We all know that you're a fast reader, but it's not like you need to rub it in our faces. Can't you just read something else?"

I didn't tell her that I had read something else—I'd read plenty of something-elses, it's just that I was greedy and I wanted even more. But the way Carolina was looking at me, it was as if I'd committed some kind of federal offense. She didn't get it. I figured that you would, and that if you said my name it would sound much nicer than when she did, but you weren't there and you didn't know my name so all I had was an annoying girl who thought she was a genius.

In case it's not obvious, Carolina isn't my favorite person.

When I didn't respond, she sighed, "Sam, you know what? You're just gonna have to wait for everyone else to catch up, since you've already read everything."

I gaped at her. "Why? Can't we just skip over some books and go to the next ones?"

"Absolutely not. We have a schedule, thank you very much. And anyway, this club doesn't revolve around you!"

It doesn't revolve around you, either, Carolina.

She didn't wait for my argument, which was going to be something about how I was the only one in that room who actually wanted to be there. Instead, Carolina turned to the nearest shelf, pulled out a random paperback, and hurled it across the table at my face. It hit me, too, because my reflexes weren't sharp enough to catch it.

The Perks of Being a Wallflower. That was the title. I'd heard of it, back when the movie came out, but I didn't know what it was about.

I eyeballed Carolina. "What do you want me to do?"

"Go sit somewhere else," she said, "and read it. We have a book to discuss."

I shrugged, because I knew they wouldn't get any discussing done, not when no one else cared. But Queen Carolina was (unofficially) in charge. And I really didn't mind leaving, really, because in all honestly I really did like it better when it was a one person book club, before the librarian saw me eating alone and thought I needed friends.

I found a place as far away from them as possible, sat down, and cracked open the book. I didn't know what to expect, but whatever I found was brilliant. You once described this feeling to me, how sometimes you skim through a page and it's like you're opening a chest of buried treasure. That's what I felt from the moment I read the first line: it was golden. Two pages in, and I'd already decided that it was my new favorite.

Chapter 7

A project for gov, a speech paper for English, and three tests (in math, science, and Spanish) to study for: that was the weekend ahead of me, and it wasn't looking pretty. Everyone said that senior year was going to be so easy. Liars, all of them.

I dragged my feet walking into the teashop, and my tennis shoes left soggy, slurred footprints in the doorway. It wasn't too crowded, which was weird, but good, because it meant there was no line for drinks.

The barista on duty was Jenny. She's small, and has a nose ring and big brown eyes and a shock of purple hair on top of her head. Jenny chews gum loudly and sticks it on the bottom of tables as she cleans them, but Krystal keeps her around because of a debt she owes to Jenny's mother, or something like that. I don't know the whole story, or if it's even true; Krystal is prone to making up those kinds of things.

"Sam, my man!" Jenny called as I shuffled up to the counter. She was always so out there, a constant beacon for attention.

I winced at her loud voice. "Hey, Jenny."

"You want the usual?"

The usual, at least for the wintertime, was peppermint tea. It was my favorite, and sounded like the perfect thing to help relieve some stress. But then I thought of you, and the very first drink I ever heard you order: vanilla bubble tea. I didn't know anything about it, really, but I found myself telling Jenny to please get me one order of that in a small mug.

She looked at me kind of funny.

I tapped my foot as I waited for my drink. There was water sloshing around in my shoes. Everything was dim and homey, and instrumental Christmas tracks were humming out of the speakers. I figured that starting on my workload would probably be a good idea, but it was sounding more appealing to just sit and think for a while, and I figured that was probably what I'd end up doing, anyway.

"One vanilla bubble tea for Sam-u-el." That was a moment later, when Jenny came out of the tiny kitchen with green-and-blue striped teacup on her palm. She was smiling; she smiled a lot. Except when she was sad, and it seemed like she was sad a lot, too.

I take back what I said about it being uncrowded. That's a lie. It was crowded, actually, it was just quiet. I saw a boy writing music, a girl sketching, a cluster of kids huddled on the couch with textbooks strewn across their legs.

But I didn't see you.

That is, not at first. Because when I was about to check the other room for a seat, I heard a psst wander into the air. It was so quiet, maybe I imagined it. Maybe it was just fate that I looked up and saw you sitting alone at a table for two, your legs crossed and a book spread under your fingertips.

I didn't think this time, didn't hesitate, and when I look back on the moment I'm proud because I didn't let my shyness get in my way. With a purpose and my backpack and a teacup in my hand, I strode over to your table and slid into the empty seat.

You didn't look up. I guess I didn't expect you to, because I wasn't surprised. I just set down my cup, pulled out the Spanish book that we were being tested on, and pretended to read. It was boring; not nearly as amazing as the book that Carolina had tried to take my head off with, which I had stayed up late into the night in order to finish. Really, I was just passing time, waiting for one of us to speak. It ended up being you.

"You know," you said. Then you paused, as if you were ending a sentence instead of beginning one. Your eyes were still scratching over a page of your book (I couldn't see the title). "You know," you continued, "we don't know each other's names. And I feel like we should, since we keep seeing each other everywhere."

You looked up at that moment, and so did I, except that I was startled and you were calm. As far as I knew, you'd only seen me once before. Unless...I felt an embarrassed flush creep onto my cheeks. A hint of a smile flickered in your eyes.

"W-when did you see me?" I questioned, too forceful. I'm not so good at nonchalance.

You smirked, just a little twitch of your lips. "Weren't you the boy at the bookstore?" You reached back and twirled the edges of your ponytail between your fingers. "The one who was messing with the magnetic poetry set?"

Red, red, redder. "Oh, um, yeah." Swallow. "That was me." I didn't know whether to be please or ashamed that you had noticed me.

"So what's your name?"

Name. What was my name again? It was stupid not to remember, but your eyes were green and that's such a nice color and maybe I didn't know you but you were so pretty and—

"Samuel Windermere," I told you. "My name is Samuel Windermere."

You raised an eyebrow. "Windermere? As in, the real estate company?"

Right. Windermere Realtors; my aunt and uncle used that company to sell their house when my sister and I moved in with them.

"Yeah, I guess so. Like that." I tried on a smile, and miraculously, you returned it.

"So, Samuel Windermere, huh?"

I nodded. "Or Sam. Just Sam."

"Just Sam," you repeated. You tasted the syllables; rolled the words over your tongue and filed them away into your memory. "I like it."

There was a teacup in front of you, a white one with blue bicycles painted on the sides. You used your pinky to twirl it around by its handle as you brushed back your hair and looked at me again.

"It's nice to meet you, Just Sam," you smirked. "I'm Ellery Eshelman."

"Oh, I know," I blurted, not thinking. Oops.

"You know?" you asked, looking confused.

"Er—yeah," I mumbled. "I—ah—saw your name on your cup at the coffeehouse in the bookstore. Ellery."

I added your name as an afterthought, and it sounded choppy and awkward but I liked the way it fell from my lips. And anyway, it made you smile. Or maybe you were smiling because I was making a weird face and you were trying not to laugh at it.

I decided to pretend it was the former.

You leaned your elbows on the table, book forgotten, and rested your chin on the backs of your hands. "That's pretty stalkerish of you, Sam," you said.

I frowned, feigning offense. "Stalkerish? Me?"

You shrugged. "I guess we could call it something else. Something prettier. Like...perspicacious?"

My heart swelled. Perspicacious: that wasn't even the right word for the situation, and you probably knew that, but it was one of my favorites. I told you so, and you grinned super wide, and suddenly we were listing all of our favorite words and I forgot that once I'd been afraid to talk to you. If I still needed any kind of reason to like you, I'd found it. Any writer girl who reads books and drinks tea and likes words is worth a strange infatuation.

The conversation gradually petered into silence, but not until after one final snippet about the books in front of us:

"What are you reading?" Me.

"The Book Thief." You. "It's good. What are you reading?"

Your mind, I thought, wishing I really could. I glanced at the cover of my book, squinted at the title even as I butchered its pronunciation terribly.

"Rayuela?" I tried, then wrinkled my nose. "It's not so good."

Shaking your head, you laughed. I laughed too, softly, even though I wasn't sure what was funny and it was more that you had one of those laughs that people call infectious. We both laughed, for a little while, before gradually becoming quiet. It was a content quiet; a happy quiet. The kind of quiet you find with best friends, not people who have known each other for barely any time at all.

We drank tea and read our books after that, and we didn't say a word. I was okay with that, though, because I would steal glances at you every few seconds. You read a lot like you wrote, with your brow knit in concentration and your lips slightly pursed. Every few moments, you'd lift your teacup to your lips, but your eyes would never leave the page.

It was nothing but a simple cup of tea shared by strangers, but to me it meant much more than that. I wasn't sure what, exactly, at the time. It felt a little bit like amazement. Maybe it was. You looked so windswept sitting there, with your fingers flipping pages and a teacup in your hand and I wanted to tell you so. But that was a weird word to use as a compliment and I didn't know how you'd take it. So I said nothing; I just watched, as usual.

You were so pretty, but I'm sorry to say that the vanilla bubble tea was awful.

Chapter 8

They say that sometimes, between two people, there's this special mental connection that's almost like a sixth sense. It's a kind of harmony, like how couples and best friends can almost read each other's minds. And maybe at that point we weren't anywhere near close enough to have that kind of perfect chemistry, but I think maybe our minds are on the same wavelength. Because on that Saturday, as I approached the big Victorian home that houses the teashop and two thrift stores, I saw you walking toward it as well, wrapped in your bright yellow raincoat.

"Sam!" you cried, noticing me at the same time that I noticed you.

I smiled and waved, squinting my eyes to see you through the misting rain. You skipped toward me, but your foot caught on the uneven pavement and you tripped, dramatically. For one frozen second you flailed through the air—before thudding, quite suddenly, into my chest.

I caught your weight with a surprised breath, then realized that you were pressed against me, clinging to my jacket to keep your balance. Your messenger bag was digging into my knee.

My face turned red; I felt it. And when you pulled away, your cheeks were pink and your eyebrows were angled and your lips were pressed together. I felt a little bit relieved, because you seemed almost as embarrassed as me.

"That was some greeting," I remarked, laughing nervously. Was that even the right thing to say? I didn't know; I was just trying to be funny. But hell, who was I kidding? I am the most unfunny person on the planet.

You laughed, though.

"Sorry about that." You half smiled, looked up from under your eyelashes, smoothed down the front of your coat. It was still raining, and we were getting soaked, but I'd almost forgotten about that.

Then: "We should probably get out of the rain," you said.

I nodded, followed you up the stairs. Turned right, then another flight, up to the teashop door. I opened the door for you, saying, "Ladies first," and you dropped a brief curtsy before slipping inside.

Krystal was working the counter that day, which is rare, because usually she just sits in the closet-sized staff room with an easel and paints. Painting is her passion; I think it's what she'd do all the time, if she didn't have the shop.

But today she was out, perched on the stool behind the counter and stringing colorful beads onto a piece of thread. She grinned when she saw us, and came around to envelope me in a cinnamon-scented hug.

"Sam, how are you?" she said, but she didn't hear my response because it was muffled by her shoulder. When she pulled back, she looked at you, and I saw you shrink a bit under the appraisal in her eyes.

Krystal is very tall, so tall that people usually think she's wearing heels. She's not; in fact, when she's in the shop, she's always barefoot. She's the kind of person who's described as devastatingly beautiful, with her dark mocha hair and cappuccino complexion, and her eyes like espresso beans. But she's kind. It's just that she has a very strong presence and that can take a while to get used to. I'm not sure if I'm used to it, and I've known her for years.

"This is Ellery," I said, awkwardly gesturing to you. "She's my—ah—friend." The way I said friend was hesitant, but it still made you smile at me. I liked the idea of making you smile.

Krystal grinned immediately; she has moods like that. "Well, I'm Krystal, and any friend of Sam is a friend of mine. He's practically royalty around here, you know."

"Oh, I don't doubt it." You laughed, tucking a strand of auburn hair behind your ear. "Prince Sam, I presume?"

I rolled my eyes. But I was smiling.

I realized, as Krystal took our orders, that I had smiled more in the days since I'd met you than I had in quite a while. And these were real smiles. Real, genuine smiles.

We sat down at a table; the same one I'd sat at when I first saw you, in fact. Somehow it was natural. Even so, it was hard not to dwell on the fact that I was sitting at a table with a beautiful girl who was beautiful in a quiet way, and that you were actually real and not a figment of my imagination.

I sipped my tea (I was back to peppermint), and watched you wrestle your netbook out of your back and set it down on the table. I watched you type, type, type yourself out of reality and into your faraway story world. And I couldn't help but ask again:

"What are you writing?"

You looked up, startled. Maybe a little annoyed. "I told you. A story."

"But what kind of story?" I pressed. "Tell me about it."

I worried; for a moment, it looked as if you were going to freeze up and shut down. Sam, you idiot, I thought. You've gone and blown it.

But then you paused. You looked down at your tea. You looked back up. You took a deep breath—and you told me everything.

I realized that usually, you were very quiet. You were like me. But this was something you loved beyond all doubt, and when given the chance, you could talk about it. I mean, really talk.

It was hard to follow you, with your quick tongue and waving hands and interwoven sentences. It was like chasing a cheetah through a maze. But it was eye-opening. You painted this—this picture inside my head, all full of colors and textures and beauty and intensity. I didn't understand it, how an entire world could be hidden inside your head. It must have been magical to live up there.

"Wow," I said, over and over and over. I used up the word, but there was feeling behind it every time. I drank in every word you said, because each one told me something more about you. And I wanted to know everything.

And then, somehow, we started talking about other things: things like school and family and books and the weather. I learned that you went to Franklin, a high school across the river. You'd moved to Portland in the summer with your family, all the way from Florida, so you didn't know the area too well. I told you that I could show you around.

Your favorite color was blue, and you commented on my blue eyes. I said that yours, in green, were pretty, and you blushed.

You loved Shakespeare; I said I hated him. That made you laugh. I told you about the book I'd just read, The Perks of Being a Wallflower, and you got really excited because it was one of your favorites. You told me that you like old musicals and country music and lace-up boots. I explained my love for comic books and action movies and everything written by Edgar Allen Poe.

We were different in a lot of ways, but I think we were very similar too. And I liked that, because we would go from arguing to agreeing and back to arguing in a heartbeat. I'd hardly known you for long, but I felt relaxed. Accepted.

You didn't get any writing done that day.

Just like the Saturday before, you had to leave quite suddenly. "Shoot, I've got to go," you murmured, abruptly ending our conversation about how nice the weather was in the winter.

"Already?" I frowned, disappointment building in my gut. An hour had passed, and I hadn't even realized. You were like Cinderella, doomed to leave the ball before the clock struck midnight. Or in this case, four P.M.

You smiled apologetically. "Yeah. I have a ballet rehearsal; The Nutcracker starts in a few days, so we're practicing like mad."

That's right. Somewhere in the whirlwind of words, you'd mentioned that you were a ballerina. It was kind of strange to imagine you doing ballet, because you were clumsy. I mentioned that, stupidly, but you just laughed. Always laughed.

"Oh, in real life, I have two left feet," you admitted. "It's different when I'm dancing." A shrug, then a mischievous smile. "And I can prove it to ya, too. My studio is in the city, and we'll have practice again tomorrow. Maybe you can drop by and watch."

My eyes grew. "I—"

"Yeah, it'll be great!" You rummaged through your bag for a pen and pencil and haphazardly scrawled out an address. "Just go to the studio and ask for Ellery at the front desk. They'll let you right in."

"Uh—" I almost objected. But then I realized that I'd be crazy to do so, and anyway, you were grinning at me so widely that I couldn't say no. I didn't want to say no.

"Sure," I said instead. I tugged the paper across the table and looked at it; the address was in walking distance of my apartment.

Your handwriting was curly and flowing. The line was ended with a tiny heart for a period.

"Great!" You shouldered your bag, somehow already packed, and tugged your raincoat tight around your shoulders. "So tomorrow, then?"

I grinned, feeling for once like I was, as a person, okay. "Tomorrow it is."

"Until then, Prince Sam," you trilled, waving over your shoulder.

As you left, Krystal came up to the table to collect our empty mugs. She paused and smiled after you, her eyebrows raised.

"New friend," she said, nodding as you opened the door.

I smiled faintly. "Yeah."

Krystal shook her head. "She's pretty."

I was glad she agreed. "Yeah," I said. "Really pretty."

"You like her?" she asked, eyeing me.

I felt my face turn bright red, and I think that was answer enough.

Chapter 9

It was Sunday. I was at the ballet studio, at the address you told me to go to, standing by the desk with my hands buried into my pockets. Stand up straight, my mind snapped. Stop looking so lost and pathetic.

I couldn't help it. That's just how I stand.

The girl at the desk didn't notice, though, or maybe she just didn't care. She hardly looked at me as she snapped out the studio name: The Pointe.

I liked that. All the studio rooms were named after different elements of ballet; The Slippers, The Tulle, The Ribbons. I didn't know much about dancing, especially not ballet, but I liked it all the same.

When I found the door, the last one on the right side of the hall, I saw that there were a bunch of people inside, boys and girls, dressed in tights and sweaters and sweats and legwarmers. Everyone was lined up along the barres, packed tight like sardines, doing those leg bends that you call pliés.

Plee-ays.

I was nervous at first, because there were so many people in there; so, so, many. But then I saw you, lifting to your toes at the barre by the window (relevé?), and that gave me enough confidence to crack the door open and slip inside.

No one looked at me, and I quickly realized that I wasn't the only spectator. There was a row of chairs alongside the door, and several of them were occupied by bored-looking teenage guys and a few eager parents. I took a seat next to a woman who was videotaping the practice on an iPad.

There was a man at the front of the room: he was young, maybe twenty-five, thereabouts, but it was obvious that he was in charge. He was counting along to the soft classical music, striding up and down the room and pausing every few seconds to adjust a dancer's position.

This was warm-up, you told me later. Every class started with work at the barre, because ballet can do terrible things to your muscles if you aren't stretched properly. That was the boring part, you said. But I didn't think it was boring. I thought it was fascinating, watching all these people moving in sync, their bodies graceful and their postures still.

The barre warm-up didn't last for long after I'd arrived, and when it ended, everyone was given a break. A flow of dancers washed away from the barres, including you. You rushed over to me, grinning, and thanked me for coming between gulps of water. There was sweat glistening on your face already, but you didn't seem embarrassed about it the way some girls are. I thought that was really cool.

You told me that your instructor's name was Grayson, and you even called him over to introduce us. He was nice, really easygoing; he smiled and even looked me in the eye when he said hello.

I met a girl, too, who came over out of nowhere as we were talking. She was really pretty, but in an obvious way. Her hair was light blonde, golden, and it was coiled into some kind of intricate bun atop her head. Your hair was in a messy twist, falling from its ribbon and into your eyes. I liked that much more.

The girl was quick to inform me that she was playing the lead role in the Nutcracker. She was Clara, and she told me that before she even gave her name. "Ellery tried for the role too, of course," she said, smiling prettily, "but the competition was so close. Plus, Ells is the sugar plum fairy, and that's a pretty good part too. Not the lead, but we can't all have what we want, right?"

She laughed. You bristled. I didn't blame you; she was very blunt.

"I'm Sam," I said awkwardly, because the only way I could think to respond was to ignore everything she had just said.

Her mouth became an O. "What a coincidence! I'm Sam, too! Well, Samantha, but everyone calls me Sam. I guess we have a lot in common, eh?" She winked at me like we shared some kind of private joke. I just wanted her to go away, because I didn't think we had anything in common at all.

You looked like you were getting mad as she stood there, trying to edge into your spotlight. Your cheeks were tinged red with anger, your lips pressed into a thin white line. I didn't like your expression; it looked like it hurt.

"I can't wait to see you dance," I said genuinely. I turned away from Samantha and tried on a smile. You came alive like Christmas lights, and a grin brightened your features. In my head, I sighed in relief. Everything felt so much better when you were smiling.

Samantha's own grin had slipped a little, but that didn't matter because just then, Grayson pulled everyone back to the floor. He called out a scene, one that he wanted to clean up, and the appropriate dancers came forward. I don't remember which it was, by name, but you were in it and that's all that mattered.

I watched as everyone tightened their shoes, adjusted their hair, and got into position. My eyes were on you as the music started.

I remembered what you had said the day before, about how you were different when you danced. And you were; I could see it quite obviously. Your eyes were confident, your movements smooth and practiced. I didn't know a lot about ballet, but I knew enough to realize that you were very good at it.

Except that "good" isn't a good enough word. You were something more like spectacular. Yeah, that fits. Spectacular is a word full of fireworks, and that's what you were as you twirled through the room on the tips of your toes. I was mesmerized by you, by your gentle beauty and the way that you held your head so high when you danced.

I think that's when I first realized that there are two sides to you: opposites, like yin and yang. On one hand, you're the clumsy girl I saw at the teashop in that awful yellow coat. On the other, you're a stunning ballerina who draws eyes to her every move. Or at least, you drew mine, and I think that counts for something.

There were plenty of other scenes practiced, but strangely, or maybe not so strangely, I only remember the ones that you were in. Sam came to me after you guys were dismissed, asked if she'd done well. I could only stare at her blankly, because I truly didn't know.

She bristled. You laughed behind your hand.

"So, what did you think?" you asked me after. We were outside the studio, walking toward the parking lot where your mom picked you up. Thank God, it wasn't raining. You were tugging your sweat-dampened hair out of its bun, your eyes shining with tired happiness.

"I thought you were amazing," I told you. I meant it. Sometimes I'm not good at seeming like I mean things, but I guess I got my point across that time because you smiled really wide and thanked me softly. Then you glanced around, your voice lowering to a conspiratorial whisper.

"And what did you think of Sam?"

I squirmed, because I was about to lie. I said, "She seems nice."

She didn't actually. She actually kind of seemed like "a downright bitch," as my sister would say. You seemed to think so too, because your eyebrow snaked up your forehead.

"Really?"

I made a face. "Well. No. Not at all, actually. I don't think I like her."

You smirked. Approval. "That's more like it." Then a sigh. "She's the biggest rumormonger I've ever met. By the end of the day, you can be certain that the entire studio will think that you're my boyfriend."

You didn't say it with disgust, just as a fact. It still made me blush, though, because I was thinking that even if they thought I was your boyfriend and it wasn't just an assumption but an actual truth, it really wouldn't be so bad at all.

I didn't say that. I just chuckled. Then I told you how good you were, again. And I meant it. Again. I felt like you needed to know.

"Thanks, Sam," you said, crossing your arms and ducking your head. You were back to that girl from the teashop again, with your little uncertainties, being swallowed up by a pair of oversized sweatpants pulled over your tights. But God, you were so pretty.

"I'm glad you came," you continued. "I—um—it means a lot, even if it was only practice."

I shook my head. "Really, it's fine. I mean, it was cool."

It wasn't just cool, it was fantastic and wonderful and that was all because of you. I berated myself in my head, because I was such a loser and I was too afraid to say all that.

We had reached the yawning mouth of the parking structure by then, and you paused, turning to face me. There was a moment of awkwardness as we just stared uncertainly at each other—then you darted forward and wrapped your thin arms around me and I hugged you back without thinking about it. Maybe it only lasted for a second, but you smelled like hot chocolate and warm vanilla and Christmas trees and everything that was winter, and that flickering moment was a beautiful eternity in my head.

"See you around, Sam," you called, pulling away and leaving me in daze. I raised a hand to wave too late; you were already darting to a green minivan with an open door. Green like your eyes.

I saw Carson Myles as I made my way home; he lives in an apartment complex near mine. He and his buddies backed me against a building, started sneering and laughing and taunting. I don't know why they do it. I found that I didn't care; I couldn't even hear what they were saying. All I could see was your face in my mind.

Before they moved on, Carson told me I smelled like a girl. He's a rumormonger too, like that girl Sam, so he says stuff like that a lot about me, tells it to a lot of people. They believe him. I care, and pretend I don't. But as I walked the rest of the way home, numbly, I couldn't help but sniff the sleeve of my sweater, just to be curious. And it smelled like you, like winter and warmth. Maybe that was your perfume.

Chapter 10

My Aunt Sheridan is not a good cook. She's not one of those aunts in books who always have pies and cookies and make elaborate dinners every night. In fact, she's really more like that hopeless mom who means well but really shouldn't be allowed in the kitchen, ever. Except that she's not my mom, she's my aunt. Regardless of what she is, though, if she ever appears within twenty feet of your refrigerator and/or stove, I suggest running for your life.

She really, truly, honestly cannot cook.

She sure thinks she can, though. She's constantly bringing home crazy recipes and ingredients, but I think she just pours everything into a bowl and puts that in the oven, because the dishes really never taste very good. Ever.

But Aunt Sheridan is nothing if not persistent. No matter how many times Uncle Dillon subtly gags on his food at the dinner table, she always keeps coming up with new poisons—I mean, meals. Sometimes I just think she's trying to spite him. Except that she forgets that I live in the house too, and I also have a taste-buds that cry out in pain whenever her cooking comes anywhere near them. Or maybe she does remember, she just doesn't care. Because that wouldn't surprise me.

On Tuesday, Aunt Sheridan came home from work with a dead body slung over her shoulder. That is, the dead body of a gigantic fish that was as big as her head and twice as thick. And she has a big head.

Apparently, she'd been watching the Food Network again, and Rachel Ray or Paula Dean or one of those people who can actually cook fried a whole fish, and now she was determined to do the same. She didn't even listen to my protest that, sometime between breakfast and dinner, I'd decided to become vegetarian and therefore couldn't eat meat.

"Sheridan, are you sure you want to try this?" That was Uncle Dillon, who was shouting into the kitchen from his permanent evening position on the recliner, watching the Ducks football game. Aunt Sheridan just clucked her tongue and said that Julia Child always took risks in her cooking, so why shouldn't she?

Julia Child this, Julia Child that. Julia Child is her idol. Julia Child was also a gourmet chef. Aunt Sheridan is not. She just likes to pretend.

I did my homework in the kitchen as she cooked, which meant spending an hour trying not to focus on the noxious smell in the air. It was easier than usual, actually, because I wasn't really doing my homework but wondering if you were doing your homework, or if you had done it already, and if your mom was a good cook because if she was, could I possibly come over for dinner everyday for the rest of high school?

By the time Aunt Sheridan called us in for dinner, I had scribbled messy circles all over my paper and done approximately half a calculus problem. I figured I probably wouldn't end up doing my math homework that night, but I didn't mind because you were much more interesting than derivatives.

Uncle Dill waddled in, grumbling and rubbing his overhanging stomach. I don't know where his gut came from, since he hardly ever touches his wife's cooking except to poke it with a fork to make sure it doesn't bite.

It smelled pretty awful in the kitchen, and while I was pretty good at pretending it didn't, Uncle Dillon is very insensitive to those kinds of things and made sure to point out the rancid aroma. Aunt Sheridan told him to sniff his shirt, because she could have sworn it was coming from him.

They love each other, really. They just have a funny way of showing it.

The food, as usual, was around ten degrees below terrible. I don't know what happened, but that fish turned into brown slop by the time Aunt Sheridan was through with it. And as for the taste? I guess if you want to describe it well, it'd be somewhere between puke-inducing and barf-worthy. Uncle Dillon made sure that was obvious, because he kept coughing and hacking every time he swallowed a bite. I just kept my head down. Sometimes my aunt forgets that I'm there and I can escape with only a half-cleaned plate.

And then sometimes, like that night, I can't.

It had been maybe ten minutes when Aunt Sheridan asked, "So, Sam. Where did you go yesterday?" and I just stared at her blankly with my half-opened mouth stuffed with food.

"Uh...on a walk?"

"Really? Because I could have sworn I saw you walking into that ballet studio down the street." She smirked. Aunt Sheridan is a professional snoop. "Are you sure there wasn't a girl involved?"

Your face flashed into my mind, flushed and smiling. Well, sure there was a girl involved, but we only hugged and that didn't mean anything really, or maybe it did, I don't know. Surely it meant something that you invited me there, but I really have no idea because girls are practically a foreign language to me.

Consequently, I said: "Um…"

"Leave the boy alone, Sher," Uncle Dill grumbled, making a face at his forkful. "He's nearly eighteen; he can do what he wants."

Aunt Sheridan doesn't let things go so easily. "But look at him, Dill, he's blushing!" she gushed. I was blushing? I wasn't trying to. I swear, sometimes it just happens. "Maybe Sam has a little crush?" She said "crush" with two syllables, a big, sneaky grin on her face.

"Or maybe," muttered Uncle Dill, "he's been poisoned by your godawful cooking."

Aunt Sheridan slapped her husband across the arm with a nearby oven mitt, and I scratched nervously at the back of my neck. Maybe, I thought, it was a little bit of both.

Chapter 11

I was really looking forward to seeing you again; it was what carried me through the school day. Even when Carson took my sandwich at lunch and smeared it across the pages of my library book, I was undeterred. (Although I did have to pay a ten dollar replacement fee, and that was kind of a downer).

I waited in the teashop for you after school with my tea and econ textbook spread out before me. There was a test in two days, and I was probably taking it less seriously than I should have, but econ is my best subject and I could handle a C.

What's with you? I asked myself as I sat there, waiting. Since when have you been willing to settle for anything less than an A?

Since I met you, I figured.

I'll admit that I got a nervous feeling in my stomach when I heard the door jingle and you rushed in, a piece of paper in your hand and your rain-frizzed hair falling into your face. I watched you call an order to Jenny at the register, then storm over to the table and dumped your bag heavily on the ground beside you. You glared at me, obviously angry.

I stared, wide-eyed, as you slammed that paper onto the wooden surface. It turned out to be a newspaper, and I couldn't see the title of the article because your hand was covering it, but whatever it was, it had you fuming. Your furious, jerky movements drew stares from around the teashop, but that was nothing new and you didn't seem to care.

"What is it?" I demanded, alarmed. The damp newspaper was leaving a dark water stain on the pages of my textbook, but I didn't move it. And you didn't move. You stood there, teeth clenched, palm pressed against newsprint.

"Ellery?"

You didn't relax, but you shifted, robotic, to reveal the heading of the article. "Gay Oregon Teen's House Vandalized." It was the front page story of the tribune, and the fine print said that it was written by someone named Max Galleger.

I understood that it was wrong, sure. No one's house should be vandalized. But I didn't understand, at first, why you were so upset about it. I guess I just kind of stared at you for a few seconds, because you stared back and then you made a kind of angry, frustrated noise and slammed into your seat.

"This boy," you snapped, "came home from school yesterday, and the word faggot was spray-painted across the front of his house. Some idiotic, rotten pieces of shit came to his house and put that terrible word on it just people that boy likes guys instead of girls." You stabbed a finger at the article, and people were watching now, really watching, but you didn't even notice because you were angry, so, so angry, more angry than I ever thought I'd see you.

"Ellery," I began.

You cut me off. "Why would somebody do this? Why would any human being ever wake up in the morning and say, 'hey, I think I'll go vandalize a gay kid's house today, because that is totally an acceptable thing to do'?" Your eyes became slits, and I leaned away. "Whoever these idiots are, they are worthless pieces of trash. Trash, Sam. I can't even explain how stupid this is. This is the kind of ridiculous thing that makes kids kill themselves."

You trailed off, into a heavy breathing silence. Jenny brought your tea, and I guess she must have heard your outburst because she looked kind of scared. She looked how I felt. Everyone was staring now, everyone within hearing distance, and that was everyone in the shop because it was that small. And their eyes were on you, not me (they probably didn't even notice me), but I could still feel them and it made me want to shrivel up into a ball and hide.

In a quiet, pathetic voice, I tried to reason with you. "Ellery, calm down. It's okay."

You slapped the table, screeched between your teeth, and leaned closer to me. Your voice dropped to a hiss.

"Is is not okay," you ground out. "Nothing like this will ever be okay. Do you know why my family moved here, Sam? Do you know why we picked up and hauled ass all the way across the freaking country?"

Your hands were shaking; your bottom lip was trembling. I shook my head quickly. Right, left. No.

"It's because eight months ago, my brother was this boy. This"—you snatched up the paper, scanned it quickly—"Joe Bergman kid was my brother, except his name was Greg. And he was gay. Openly, because he wasn't afraid of the label or of himself. My parents are super Catholic, and maybe they didn't love that but they loved him, so they were okay. I was okay. My other siblings were okay. But the kids at his school were not okay, and they tormented him to the point that he didn't want to be here anymore. He didn't tell us, but they were teasing and bullying him and it tore him apart until it was too much. And by then, it was too late for any of us to do anything because he was already gone."

A sob. A choking sob to end your sentence, and your hand flew over your mouth. And then there was silence. It was the worst silence I had ever endured, because it was painful and heavy and full of unspoken words.

"Ellery, I—"

"He was fourteen, Sam." You were pressing your nails into the palm of your hand. "He was only a freshman in high school, and he killed himself because idiots like these wouldn't let him alone. And then we left, we just left, because none of of could stand being near the people that had made him do it."

Your eyes, they were elsewhere, far away, and it was scaring me. Ellery, I wanted to say, come back. Please. But when you did return your focus, there was so much pain in your green irises that I just wanted you to look away again. It hurt me that you were hurt, and it was more than just that automatic human compassion instinct. I cared about you. I hardly knew you, but I cared about you, and I didn't like how upset you were.

"I don't understand," you whispered. "I don't understand how people can do things like this"—you waved the article—"and be okay with themselves. It's disgusting. And wrong. And it needs to stop, but I know it never will because this is just human nature and that's never going to change."

You were on the verge of tears. I could hear it in your breaking voice; I could see the moisture shimmering, the tiny teardrop that slipped to the corner of your eye. Inside, I was panicking. I didn't know how to handle a normal girl, much less one who was crying. But you were trying not to cry, I could tell. You'd finally realized how many spectators you had, and you were biting down on your hand to keep away the tears.

I wanted to say so many things to you in that beat of silence, and if I was able to organize my thoughts better, I swear that I would have. I wanted to tell you that I knew how you felt; I knew how much it hurt to lose someone and I would listen to you because sometimes pain hurts less if you share the burden. I wanted to tell you that I knew this was wrong, because fourteen-year-olds should not be killing themselves and kids with spray paint should not be vandalizing boys' houses for being different.

And I wanted to say that I knew, that I understood, that a boy could love a girl or a girl could love a girl or a boy could love a boy because it was love, and that was what truly mattered. People didn't see it like that a lot of the time, and I ached to tell you how that made me sad, how it made me sad to see that it made you sad too, and really I just wanted to make you feel better more than anything.

But words don't come to me like they come to you, and all the thoughts in my head were a mess. Such a mess, always a mess. For once, it had nothing to do with the fact that you were a pretty girl, it's just that I couldn't sort out my feelings because these were emotions and I wasn't any better than those than I was with words.

I looked at you, sitting there doe-eyed and quivering, collapsing under the weight of your rigid beliefs, and I wanted to say all those things so badly. But I couldn't. I'm pathetic. I could only reach across the little table and gently pull your clenched fists away from your face and lay them down on the wood.

"I'm sorry," I said, my palms on your fingers. Your hands were cold, shaking. "I'm so sorry."

It was weak. I could apologize all I wanted to, but I knew that it wouldn't matter because this wasn't my fault. I knew because that's how I felt a few years ago when I was the one that people were saying I'm sorry to.

Your eyes dropped, dimming slightly, and your lips curved slowly downward. Disappointment. You were disappointed in me.

I didn't blame you. I was disappointed in me, too.

Chapter 12

I worried through the next school day, thinking about you. You'd left quickly the day before, and you had been so out of it that your tea was left sitting on the table, untouched. I didn't know where you lived, I didn't have a number to call, and I had no idea whether or not you were okay.

I hoped you were.

My aunt called after school, last minute, and said that she was being held up at work and couldn't come pick me up. That meant walking home.

It was raining again. Great.

My teachers had been going on all day about how it was 12/12/12, and wasn't that so special, and did you hear about that one kid in that one city who turned twelve today at 12:12:12? It didn't feel special, especially not when I was footing it through puddles on the city streets and getting soaked because I left my stupid umbrella on my bed. I couldn't wait to get home and be dry and warm—even the prospect of doing homework was sounding appealing.

But you know that tendency I have, to stare at my feet as I walk and just kind of go along instead of paying attention to where I'm going? Well, I was doing that. Again. As usual. And by the time I actually looked up because I was wondering why it was taking so long to get home, I was nearing 23rd, over halfway to the teashop. I guess my feet knew what I really wanted, although I couldn't decide whether what I wanted was to drink tea or have the possibility of seeing you.

Regardless, I was standing there in the rain and people were shoving past me and I figured that it was a bit too late to turn back now.

I didn't think I'd be seeing you at the teashop, not after how upset you'd been the previous day, but I still hoped you might be there as I made my way up the stairs. My hand was on the door when a cough came from behind me, and I nearly jumped out of my skin.

I turned. You were standing there, a few steps down, being dwarfed by a gigantic maroon-and-white striped sweater that hung halfway to your knees. Your hair, pulled up into a ponytail, was twisted around your fingers.

"Hey, Sam," you said quietly.

I forgot to speak for a moment, because you were there, actually there, right in front of me. "Hey, Ellery," I managed after a moment. "You—uh, you going in?"

You chewed on your bottom lip, deliberating, and stared at the door behind me. I wondered if you were thinking about your outburst, and how all the regulars who had heard it would be there again, and they would stare at you and judge you and that would hurt, even if you weren't as insecure as me.

You shook your head no.

"Actually, I was thinking..." Pause. You licked your lips. "I was thinking that maybe I could take you up on that offer of yours."

I frowned. "Offer?"

"A few days ago, you said you'd show me around, since I'm new here and stuff." You tucked a stray strand of hair behind your ear. "Are we still on for that?"

"O-oh, of course!" I stuttered. "Yeah, definitely, um…" I scratched my head as you watched with a sliver of a smile. "Where do you want to go?"

You shrugged, carefree. Your features broke into a surprising grin, and it was like the sun slicing through a cloud cover after a rainy day. "I dunno," you singsonged. "On an adventure?"

We ended up at Couch City Park on Glisan, trying to squeeze under your child-sized umbrella. It didn't work very well because of my height, so I ended up having to carry the bright pink canopy to shield us both. My backpack was weighing me down, but I was okay with pain in my back because you were beside me, and as cheesy as it sounds you were smiling and laughing and that just made me happy.

You didn't mention anything about that article or your brother, so I didn't say a word either. That was a conversation for another day. But you did mention the day's current date as we strolled, side by side, down the sidewalk.

"It's kind of sad," you mused. "I mean, this is the last time that we'll ever see this same pattern for the whole rest of the century. That's a long time. And when I think about how all these other dates have passed, and how it's been twelve whole years into this century and I've been alive to see all of them, but I probably won't be around for the next set, it's—it's just kind of flooring, you know? Because there have been so many days and months and years and there will be a ton more of them to come. And someday, someone is going to be looking back on us as history, because we'll be the past, and really, when you think about it, this one day is so insignificant in the long run, but to us, to everyone right now, it's such an amazing and crazy and beautiful moment. But there have been other centuries, and other 12/12/12s, and there will be more and more and more, and really, we're just a blink of the universe's eye. At the end of the day, we really mean nothing."

I looked at you, awestruck. You were standing there, crossing your arms over your chest and staring at the floor with a shocked expression, and you looked like such a normal girl. But all the words that had just come out of your mouth—those weren't normal, and I guess that meant that you weren't either.

"That's not true," I said firmly, surprising myself, because you were looking small and disheartened and I wanted to see you smile. "We don't mean nothing, Ellery. We exist, and we're real, and we're on Earth and living in it and doing beautiful and terrible things, every single person alive. There's no such thing as insignificance, because we're all here, contributing to the whole big picture. Even if we're not doing much, we are, just because we exist. And I think that should count for something."

You froze there for a moment, stopping completely in your tracks. With your hands on your hips, you stared pensively at the pavement. I toed at the ground; had I said something wrong? Then, suddenly, you turned to me, and you were beaming.

"Yeah," you said slowly. "Yeah. Samuel Windermere, you are absolutely right!" The smile on your face was huge as you murmured, sincerely, "Thank you."

I grinned back. You returned to what I had come to think of as your default setting, smiling and clever and just a little bit closed off. But that was okay. Because for a fraction of a second, maybe unintentionally, you'd let me see inside your mind. It was absolute discord in there. And it was absolutely beautiful.

Chapter 13

At breakfast on Thursday morning, Aunt Sheridan told me that we were going to start Christmas decorating the next day. She had big plans, to buy all new Christmas decorations and a tree from one of the farms outside of the city.

"People in other states are begging for Oregon's Christmas trees," she informed me. "And we have them right here."

Uncle Dillon mumbled and grumbled through his morning routine, but I caught him half-smiling when my aunt had turned away. He would never admit it, but whenever Aunt Sheridan was excited about something, he couldn't help but feel the same way, too. And that, I think, is love.

"Sam, if you want to invite any of your friends to help out, that would be okay," my aunt added as I was putting my empty cereal bowl into the sink. She said it as if maybe things had suddenly changed and I actually did have friends and didn't spend lunches alone in the corner of the cafeteria. The look on her face was so hopeful that I couldn't help but nod and give a halfhearted sure, even though I knew it wasn't happening. If I couldn't amass a positive number of friends in nearly eighteen years of life, there was no way that I'd come up with one in less than a day.

I didn't really mind, though, the way I usually did when my aunt inadvertently brought up my lack of friends. I was too busy trying to hide a smile, because I'd spent nearly the whole afternoon with you the day before. And at the end of it all, when we'd circled back to the teashop and your mom was coming to pick you up, you gave me your number.

Seven digits and an area code. Right there, in my phone, right beneath a picture I'd snapped of you as you were saying goodbye. And it was real. A real girl, one who I really, truly liked, had given me her number. You had given me your number.

The thought kept me smiling all day.

I spent my classes checking my phone every five seconds, as if there was even half a chance that you would call me in the middle of calculus for no reason and we'd hold a conversation over Mr. Kuroda's droning lesson on logarithms. You didn't, of course.

I didn't expect you to. The fact that you'd spoken first, said the words I couldn't, asked for my number then gave me yours, didn't mean anything, really. I'd pretty much given up by the end of the day, because let's face it, I was too shy and too lame to make the first move, even though, as a guy, I think that was what I was supposed to do.

Naturally, when my phone rang as I was at my locker, I thought it was my aunt, because no one else would call me, really. But it wasn't Aunt Sheridan's name on my screen; it was your face, your smiling face.

"Hello?" I breathed into the receiver, hardly daring to believe it. I was leaning against the side of my open locker to steady myself, because my legs were almost knocked out from under me when you responded.

"Hey, is this Sam?" you asked, a smirk in your voice.

In the background, I heard chattering, conversation, laughter. "Uh—uh, yeah. Is this, er, Ellery?"

You laughed. "Who else would it be, silly?"

I didn't know—why did I ask that question? But I just laughed too, because I'd come to realize that with you, a laugh was almost always okay.

"So, why are you calling?" I asked, not thinking about it. "I mean, not that I didn't want you to call or anything, because I did—but not like that, I mean, I just wanted you to...uh..."

Idiot.

"I just wanted to make sure this was the right number," you explained, chuckling. Your voice sounded different on the phone, as voices always do, but it still had that ever-present hint of teasing. I could practically see you there, smiling, leaning against your own locker. I didn't understand how you managed it, smiling all the time. I certainly couldn't do it.

It occurred to me then, as I pulled out a few books and closed my locker, that maybe you could be the friend that Aunt Sheridan wanted me to invite for the next day's events. Asking you over would be an even bigger leap than talking to you was—but I had hurdled that, and there was a small flicker in my mind that said I could pass this, too.

"Hey, Ellery?" I said, shifting the phone in my hand.

"Hey, Sam?"

"Um..." Come on man, don't chicken out now. Just say it. "So, we're Christmas decorating at my house tomorrow and my aunt said I could invite a friend and I don't know if we're friends but I think we might be so I was wondering if you maybe wanted to help?"

I said it all way too fast, in a big messy rush. But it was out and in the air now, and I was almost kind of proud because I'd actually found the guts to ask.

"Christmas decorating, huh?" You paused. My brain fretted that you'd sounded skeptical, maybe I'd crossed over a line, and dear God what if you said no, and—

"Sounds fun," you said. "I'm in."

My hand was on my closed locker. People were passing, moving, not noticing me standing there, frozen. Disbelieving.

"Wait... Really?"

A trickling laugh. "Yes."

"Yes?"

"Yes, Sam!" you cried, giggling.

I must have sounded like a complete idiot, but that was okay. I had asked you out on a...a date? No, it wasn't a date, not really, it couldn't be, not when my aunt and uncle were there too. But it was something, that's for sure, and since that was more than nothing I figured that something was a pretty good place to start. Especially because you'd said yes.

Yes.

Yes.

Chapter 14

That was, I decided, the perfect word to describe how I felt on Friday afternoon, swimming in apprehension while parked outside your house. Aunt Sheridan, in the driver's seat (she always insisted on driving), was complimenting your house. It was one of those pretty, big Victorians that she wishes we could afford. Uncle Dillon was shushing her, saying that she was talking so, so loud and could she please calm down because he was trying to hear the radio.

And I was dumbstruck. Dumbstruck because this was real, and we were actually at your house and you were going to be outside any second now. Dumbstruck because of the solemn words trickling from the backseat speakers.

"One of the worst school shootings in American history…"

I didn't want to think about it anymore.

Thank God, Uncle Dill changed the channel to Christmas music, and at the same time you came dashing outside in an apple-red sweater with a giant reindeer on the front. I leaned across the seat to open the door for you, and you climbed inside with a greeting and a smile.

"Hi, Mr. and Mrs. Greenwood," you said. "Thank you for inviting me; it's so nice to meet you."

Uncle Dill smiled a bit and waved at you, and Aunt Sheridan twisted all the way around to reach out and shake your hand. Her blonde hair was wild, a frizzy mane around her head, but she was bright-eyed and beaming and so were you.

"You must be Ellery," she gushed. "Please, call me Sheri. And look at you, such a pretty girl!" You turned the same color as your sweater and smiled as Aunt Sheridan confided, "Sam really likes you, you know."

"Aunt Sheridan," I hissed, appalled.

But you just laughed, your cheeks a glowing shade of rosy pink. "I really like him too," you smirked.

Aunt Sheridan went crazy at the Christmas tree lot, as expected, because there were so many trees and she had to find the one that was just perfect. I thought they all looked the same, but maybe that was just me.

You walked beside me, hands buried in the pockets of your jeans, as my aunt darted through the aisles and past crates of trees and called out names and prices in her too-loud voice. The smell of pine crept up my sweater and through my hair and into my nose, tickling my senses.

"How about this one, Ellery?" called my aunt from around the corner. She had taken a liking to you already, I could tell.

We approached Aunt Sheridan, who stood beside her husband with her hands extended toward the most awful-looking tree I had ever seen. It was flocked, like the pretty white ones that look like snow, except that this was bright pink and terrible and looked like something had gone very wrong.

"It looks like moldy cotton candy," I said, raising an eyebrow.

Uncle Dillon grunted. "Or furry intestines."

And you: I saw your face twist up, your nose wrinkling as you tried to keep a look of disgust off of your features. "Um, it's...colorful?" you offered.

I shook my head, smirking, and my uncle snorted. "Ellery, please, don't try to spare my wife's feelings. If you don't like the tree, don't hesitate to say so."

Aunt Sheridan shot him a poisonous glare, and you still hesitated. You were too nice then, you're too nice now, and all you could manage was a sheepish shrug and a mouthed apology. My aunt waved it off, tossed back her hair, and waddled along to the next set of trees. I began to follow, but quickly realized that you weren't next to me and turned around.

You were standing there, hands in your pockets, your boots dusted in green pine needles. Your eyebrows were knit tight, your eyes pointed downward and your expression kind of bittersweet.

"Ellery?" I murmured, worried.

You looked up immediately, startled, and your eyes met mine. "Oops, daydreaming," you laughed nervously. "Sorry, about that, I'm fine."

We ended up with a Noble fir, because Aunt Sheridan claimed that Douglas trees had weak boughs. I think she read that on the internet, because I swear I still couldn't see the difference.

She'd spent all day buying new decorations, and they were strewn all around the apartment when Uncle Dillon and I hauled the tree up the elevator and squeezed it through the front door. Boxes of booby traps covered the floor, so that we were forced to dance over all the mess on tiptoes. That was easy for you, ballerina, and you even managed to look pretty and graceful while skipping past ornaments and garlands.

"Put it right here, Dill!" Aunt Sheridan called, over in the living room. The six foot tree was placed next to our fireplace, and even though it was a little bit lopsided it looked so festive and beautiful and it made the whole room smell like Christmas.

Uncle Dillon strung lights. Aunt Sheridan made hot chocolate (from a box, so it actually tasted good). You and I danced around the room, dangling ornaments from the tree and putting wreaths above doorways and singing along to the Christmas songs that played from the TV. At one point when you were hanging a garland on the fireplace mantle, you slipped off the step stool and I caught you and we both ended up tangled in that garland, laughing.

It all felt so comfortable. Being around you was so natural that I couldn't help but hope in the back of my mind that maybe that meant we were meant to be. You were a newly discovered star, a dazzling young light that was caught so perfectly in the night sky. And with your hair flowing behind you, untamed, your beautiful ugly Christmas sweater, and your rosy cheeks dusted with glitter from the snowflake ornaments, I thought you were as flawless as a person could be. I couldn't take my eyes off you.

But every now and then, I'd glance over at you when you thought no one was looking, and you'd just be standing there with this blank stare and unstrung decorations in your fists. And in those little moments, I guess you just looked sad.

"Would you look at that," Aunt Sheridan enthused, smiling. The finished product of the evening's work lay before us. The living room was done up in garlands and wreaths and twinkling colored lights, and the bright pinpoint bathed us in a transparent glow. The tree-topper star smiled down at us.

Even Uncle Dill grinned and admitted, "It looks great. You kids did good."

"Yeah," I agreed, mesmerized.

And then you were the only one left to give your opinion; except that you didn't, you were so quiet despite being right there beside me, and even though we waited for a moment you said nothing so I just glanced over—

There were tears streaming down your face.

I gasped softly, which drew your attention, and then you were swiping, swiping, swiping at your eyes and murmuring apologies behind your hand. But you didn't stop crying.

"I'm sorry," you mumbled helplessly as I stood there, dumbstruck once again. "Oh God, I'm so sorry."

"No, no, sweetie, shh," said Aunt Sheridan, looking shocked. Uncle Dill was already backing out of the room. "I'll go and make some more hot chocolate, all right?" No one answered her. "All right."

Then she was gone too, and it was just me, you, and your white diamond tears.

"Ellery," I tried, very gently. "Ellery, what's wrong?" I reached out, carefully put my palm on your arm as you pressed your face into your hands. Your shoulders were shaking, sending silent tremors through my arm.

You looked up. Your tears, wet and fresh, left tracks on your cheek that glistened in the lights as you stared at the tree. At the floor. At anything but me.

"I'm sorry," you repeated. You shook your head, bit your fist, pulled it away. "I was just thinking—about this, and...and how lucky I am to be standing here right now with you in front of all these beautiful decorations, but at the same time twenty-seven people on the other side of the country are dead in an elementary school and—"

Your voice caught in your throat, and you paused. I watched your face, the planes in shadows, as you attempted to collect yourself and your thoughts. When you continued, you sounded so small.

"Twenty kids are dead, Sam. Twenty little kids who didn't do anything but go to school, and seven teachers who were just trying to do their jobs. And I just keep thinking about how those kids aren't going to see this Christmas, they aren't going to get visits from Santa Claus, their families are going to spend the holidays grieving because their children are gone forever—and I'm here, perfectly fine and lucky, and it's not fair and it feels wrong."

"Wrong," I repeated hollowly.

"Wrong," you agreed. "Wrong because those people are dead and I'm in the middle of such beautiful things. People were mourning while I was here, laughing and smiling and being happy. The parents of those children and the families of those teachers aren't happy. And they probably won't be for a long time, because the people they love are just gone.

"It hurts so much to lose someone, Sam. Especially when they're so young, when they have futures ahead of them and lives they could have lived and it's suddenly all over, because of one monster with a gun. One man. Killed twenty-seven people. Twenty-seven boys and girls and men and women are never going to open their eyes again. And their families—their families are all left here in pieces because now there's a hole in their lives and it's never going to be truly fixed, not ever. There are dozens of childless parents who aren't going to see their kids grow up, and I don't even know if you understand but I just can't, Sam, I—"

Your breath hitched at the end, dissolving into a sob that shook through your whole body, and I was just standing there thinking a million things at once and trying not to combust. It was your empathy, your overwhelming feeling for these people that you didn't even know, that got me the most. Because here you were, crying and pouring out this river of emotion in earnest, and you felt so much and you were so much that it was like a knife twisting in my gut, making my pain your pain, making our pain twist into one entity that lived and breathed within both of us and connected us by heartstrings.

And I understood—I did. I understood the pain of losing someone, and how even though time passes it just doesn't go away. I knew what you meant, about the parents. Because my aunt and uncle, they were childless, technically. They never had children and maybe didn't want to, but they ended up without a choice because of the crash and my parents and me and my sister coming to live with them because they were really all we had. But they love us, and I knew that if I was one of those kids, they would be that woman in the picture on the news, the one with the phone who was crying and screaming and looking so completely broken. Even if they're not real parents, even if they're adoptive parents or step parents or other family members, a parent should never lose their child like that. Not ever.

I wanted to tell you that, so badly. And this time, I did. I whispered it into your ear as I put a hand on your back and led you to the couch to sit, because you were shaking so hard that I didn't know if you could hold yourself up.

"Thank you," you whispered, rubbing your arms and huddling into the cushions. "I'm sorry, I-I don't know what's wrong with me, I shouldn't be so dramatic..." I peered at you carefully as you pinched the bridge of your nose. It seemed like you were done for the moment, so I cleared my throat.

"You know, I was in study hall when I found out today," I said softly. "I was on the computer in the library, and the article was on the home page, and I turned to the girl at the desk next to me and told her that someone had just opened fire at a school in Connecticut. And she just looked at me with this weird face and said, 'So? What's in Connecticut?' and I don't understand how people can't care about something like this. And the same thing, with the mall in Happy Valley. I was just at Clackamas with my aunt last week, and two people died there. It was right near home, too, but no one seemed to care. And I just—I guess what I'm trying to say is that I get it, Ellery. I really do. I know how it hurts an how it feels wrong, 'cause it is wrong. But"—I took a deep breath—"that doesn't mean that you should beat yourself up about it, because it wasn't your fault. And maybe today you were happy, but you shouldn't feel bad about it, not like this. You're an amazing person, Ellery, and the best thing you can do for these people is to continue being what you are and keep beauty in the world.

I let air out in a long rush, feeling the finished words swarm out of my mouth and cling to the walls. Out. Done. It was the most I'd said to you at once. It was the most I'd said in a while. And there you were, looking at me with teary eyes and red tracks on your cheeks, and you looked so strained and heartbroken but also hopeful and strong, and the contradiction of it was painful and soothing, both at once. I wanted to kiss you, at that moment, but I knew I couldn't because that wasn't what you needed. Right now, I could see it in your eyes: you needed a hug.

So I drew you into my chest, head against shoulder and sweater against sweater, arms wrapped around each other in an embrace of comfort and warmth and everything that was okay but wasn't, at the same time. And it didn't make sense, but nothing seemed to right then.

We sat there for an eternity, maybe more, but it didn't feel too long. It felt right, as we shared warmth and sorrow and everything, spoken and unspoken, and most of all tried not to think about it.

About an elementary school in a state all the way across the country. About childless parents. About murdered children and teachers. About twenty-seven eyes that would never open again.

Chapter 15

We're really lucky in America, they always say, because we have so many rights and we can do so many things and there are places in the world that don't have that luxury. And I know that. Really, I do. But one of those right certainly can't be to walk into a school and shoot little kids.

Everything you said made me think—really made me think—and after you left, when it was late at night, I just lay in bed and thought for hours, wide awake. I wondered why someone would ever believe themselves entitled to commit a crime so terrible; I thought about how fragile life really is. And I decided that man, whoever he was and whatever walk of life he came from, was one of two people: he either didn't understand how breakable human beings are—or he did, completely, and just didn't care.

Thinking about it all made me angry. Really angry, angry like I was when that bus driver showed up at our doorstep with his condolences, and when that boy broke my sister's heart when she was eighteen. It was the kind of anger that you feel when someone close to you gets hurt, except that I didn't know these people or that man. But that didn't change the way I felt, did it?

It was sad, too. Sad because I'd been trying so hard since I met you to believe that maybe people were good, and things weren't lost. But I didn't understand people, and why they did awful things, so how could I decide that for sure?

It was always harder to think positively at two A.M., and harder to find goodness when there were human beings in the world who were so bad.

I felt swallowed whole by the next morning, running on half an hour of almost-sleep. As I sat there, hair sticking up, shirt wrinkled, I wondered if you were any better. You'd left the evening before still teary-eyed, but at least you were wearing a watery smile.

As I went through the typical Saturday morning routine, I thought about calling you, since that seemed like the kind of thing a concerned friend should do. But you ended up calling me before I could finish debating, just as I was rinsing off my plate of hastily scrambled eggs.

"Hello?" I answered quickly, balancing my phone between my ear and shoulder. "Ellery?"

"Hey, Sam," you said, sounding tired. Maybe you had gotten as little sleep as me. You yawned between syllables. "I'm at the bookstore right now, the one on Burnside, and I wanted to talk so I was wondering if you'd meet me there?"

As if you even needed to ask. I said of course, sure, if I hurried I could be there in twenty minutes. You laughed a bit at my stumbling sentences, and that was so relieving because you weren't crying.

After I hung up and put my plate in the sink, I dashed through the living room, toward the hallway. The tree and lights were dormant now, dim, but I saw them still as they were the night before: beautiful, tragic, illuminating your tears.

You were at a table in the cafe, just like I'd seen you all those days ago, except this time you were waiting from me. You looked up from your book when I approached and sat down, then shoved a paper cup to me across the surface. There were two of them, and you had the other.

"I don't know if you drink coffee," you admitted, blushing sheepishly, "so I just got you a cappuccino and hoped for the best."

I smiled. "This is fine, thanks."

I hated cappuccinos.

I drank it anyway.

We made idle chitchat for a while, discussing the lightest, most trivial topics we possibly could, until finally your lips curled up into a little smile and you reached into the purse balanced on your lap. When you pulled out your hand, there were three little pieces of paper between your fingertips. You slid them across the table.

"My family really wants to meet you," you told me.

I swallowed, glancing warily at the papers. "Really?"

You nodded vigorously and pointed at the little slips. "My studio's performance of The Nutcracker starts tomorrow night, and those are three tickets for the seven o'clock show. For you, your aunt, and your uncle. You'll have seats right in the front row with my parents."

Tickets. Performance. Seats. Parents.

Why does it matter that she wants you to meet her parents, Sam? I asked myself. It's only a problem if you're her boyfriend, which you aren't.

I wished I was.

"Well, Ellery, I—"

"Pleeease come, Sam! My family is looking forward to it, and it would mean a lot to me if you were in the audience."

I looked at the tickets. Seven P.M. Sunday, December fifteenth. Keller Auditorium. I tried to imagine my aunt and uncle there, in such a nice place; Aunt Sheridan in lime-green sweatpants, Uncle Dill with his unshaven face. It just didn't fit.

But then I looked at you, really looked at you. I saw your smirk, one side of your lips pulling up and cratering a dimple in your cheek. And your hair, wavy and careless, slipping into your face. You usually wore makeup, but you didn't that day, so I could see the way your eyes were still rimmed with telltale red.

And God, you were so beautiful.

"Well?" You reached across the table, wrapped your soft hands around mine, and gave me a look that told me this was real, and it would really mean a lot to you if I went and saw your show.

How could I say no?

As I accepted the tickets, telling you that I couldn't wait and also trying not to worry about my oddball family, I felt some of that inner balance return. The world still wasn't good; it wasn't anywhere close. There was so much bad, so many bad things and people and places and events—but you were good. You were full of purity and morality, and you had a kind heart and a beautiful soul. I realized it quite clearly in that flicker of a moment.

The world wouldn't ever be good, not completely. It was sad, sure. It was true. But you: you had goodness, loads of it. And that thought was enough to get me through the day.

So maybe, I figured, if I was thinking about you, thinking a lot wasn't such a bad thing after all.

Chapter 16

I don't know a lot about dancing, especially not ballet. Everyone in my family has two left feet, even though my sister went through a phase where she thought she'd become a famous hip-hop dancer. We went to see her show, and every step looked like she'd been electrocuted with every movement. But we still gave her flowers and told her she was great. She quit after one season. She's always been fickle that way.

But that's beside the point. You're a much better dancer than my sister. It's just that I felt strange, being in the auditorium among all the well-dressed parents and family members, even though I'd dug up nice clothes and Aunt Sheridan was wearing quiet colors and Uncle Dillon even shaved, and pretending that this was my sister's recital in her dinky middle school auditorium helped me feel less overwhelmed.

I have this really bad habit of thinking that everywhere I go, people are watching me and judging me and scheming up ways to make me miserable. Don't take it the wrong way, because it's not like I thought that about your family, but when I saw your mom and dad and little sister and older sister and two older brothers, I couldn't help the immediate fear that they were going to absolutely hate me.

You always bother me about that; you say that I should expect people to treat me well because that's what I deserve and if I believe that, it's what I will receive. But you hadn't told me that back then, so my stomach was twisting when your dad shook my hand.

"Nice to meet you, Sam," he said, smiling at me. He had salt-and-pepper hair and kind gray eyes. "You're Ellery's..."

An open-ended question, empty for me to fill in. "Um, friend," I supplied, resisting the urge to scratch at my neck. "Nice to meet you, Mr. Eshelman."

He didn't tell me to please call him by his first name. I guess he wasn't the type, and neither was your mom. But she was very nice, and she patted my arm as she said hello in a perfectly motherly way that made my gut twist. Her red hair was loud, but it was pulled back into a solemn bun, and she had green eyes like you.

Your brothers, Ed and Evan, weren't as enthusiastic, but I guess that was their job because if I had a little sister I'd be the same way. Emma was nineteen, two years older than you, but she was shorter and had to crane her neck to look me in the eye. She's the kind of sharp girl who catches eyes and breaks hearts, just like my sister. I think they'd get along well.

"Hm, guess Elle was right," she said, before even introducing herself. "You are cute."

I guess you're not the only girl in your family who likes making me blush.

Then the only person left was your little sister, who was seven and clinging to your mom's pants, her blonde head peeking around at me.

"This is Erica," said Evan, shooing her into the open. She stared at me for a brown-eyed moment, then dashed over and wrapped her little arms around my legs.

"Hello, Erica," I greeted her. She gave me a gap-toothed grin. It was always so much easier to talk to little kids than adults.

My aunt and uncle decided to step forward and introduce themselves then. At least my aunt did, because she can't handle being silent for more than ten seconds at a time.

"I'm Sheridan," she boomed, too loud as always. I winced, but your parents only smiled placidly and shook her hand. "And this is my husband, Dillon. It's so nice to meet you."

"Same, same," said your mother. "Ellery told us how much she likes you all, and she's really glad to have you all here. She won't be out until after the show, but I know she'll be looking for you in the audience."

I smiled at that, hoping it was true.

Ed, your eldest brother, approached me as we made our way through the crowd to our seats, pulling me back from the group. I'm tall, but he's even taller, and even though he has kind eyes he also has a way of looking down his nose at people.

"So, Sam." He clapped me on the back, a little too hard. "I guess you're dating my sister?"

In my dreams. "Uh, no, I'm not. We're, uh, just friends."

He raised an eyebrow, gave me a once over, and elbowed me in the arm. "But you want to, eh?" When I didn't respond right away (my throat had gone dry), he chuckled. "Just admit it, kid. You like Ellery, it's plain as day."

I swallowed. "Well, um, yeah, I—"

"Knew it!" he chortled, pumping a fist. He was smirking, but in a weird way where his top lip curled up almost like a sneer. Later you told me that's because he got hit really hard in the face with a baseball when he was a kid, and the stitches make him smile weird. But I could tell his intentions were good, even though when he slapped my back again, it still hurt.

"Well, kid," he declared, punching my shoulder lightly, "I guess that's all right. Seems to me like the two of you would work out just fine."

And I just laughed, nervously, because that's all I could think to do, even though I was beaming inside.

Our families are direct opposites, you know; yours is poised and together, mine is casual and scattered. But maybe it's true what they say about opposites attracting, because my aunt and your mom clicked instantly, and our dads even got to talking about their shared love for football. And maybe I didn't become best friends with your brothers and your little sister was the only one who talked to me, but I was there for you, and you should know that when the curtain rose, I was the most excited person in the room.

Everything was so spectacular, and I was blown away. I guess I'm supposed to like watching football and sports, but I thought the dancers were more impressive than any traditional athlete. There were music and lights and props and dancers, and I saw Samantha who was good, but not nearly as good as you when you finally waltzed on stage.

Erica, who told me that she was a ballerina in training, spent most of the time proudly whispering the names of movements into my ear. I listened at first, because I admittedly wanted to be able to impress you after the show with something like your pirouettes were amazing (which they were), but the second I actually saw you, Erica's words turned to much in my mind.

The girl on stage, costumed in a jeweled pink tutu and sparkling tiara, was not you. But she was, and she—you—was beautiful. You were a completely different person on stage; head high, glittering smile, hair secured and face painted. You were royalty of the highest stature, and I'd never seen anyone so stunning in my life.

Every single move you made left me speechless, because you were so graceful and elegant and you weren't you but you were you, you were the you-est I'd ever seen you. It didn't make any sense, but I knew if I told you, you'd understand.

I'd been reading before I went to the show, and in my book there was a word that I'd never seen or heard before in my life. Terpsichorean. It was a strange word, foreign on my tongue, but at the same time it was perfect because of what it meant.

Terpsichorean. As a noun, it means a dancer. It meant you. And I think that it described you better than simply saying "dancer," because you were so much more. That word is full of letters and syllables and when you look at it, it's chaotic and dizzying.

You were dizzying. Watching you twirl made my head spin, but in the best way possible. You were a whirlwind of pink and white and glitter, and you had so much life in every motion that I was left in awe. Even when I felt an irrational stab of jealousy when you danced your partner piece (pas de deux, Erica said), with that boy who you swore swore swore is gay, I was mesmerized. I didn't understand how you could move about on complete tiptoe for so long, and still look completely overjoyed.

And the look on your face—it was more than just a smile. It expressed your complete love for what you were doing, and it made me love you for loving something so much, even though that something wasn't me.

I bought you flowers in the lobby after the show, and they were just tulips but the lady selling them said that giving tulips to a person after their performance means you cherish them and their dancing, and I did cherish you. They were red, the same color as your painted lips, and when I gave them to you, you threw your arms around me, tutu and all, and squealed.

I couldn't stop smiling because you liked them, and you couldn't stop smiling because you were just happy, I guess, and we just stood there smiling at each other until your family came round and congratulated you as well.

Your fellow performers came out as well, and you gave each other thumbs-up signs. I tried to remember the right terms for the moves you'd done, but I couldn't so I just settled for telling you that you were perfect. And you were—you really were.

When I said that, you flushed and giggled and buried your face in the bouquet. I could have stood there and watched you forever, with your eyes drifting shut and the flowers to your lips, but your mom called you to go too soon because it was late and there was school the next day. Before you left, you hesitated—then you tiptoed toward me and brushed your lips against my cheek.

"Thanks for coming, Sam," you said. "Really, thank you. I'll see you later, yeah?"

I was frozen, my hand on my cheek, and I could only stare after your retreating form as it disappeared into the crowd.

And I decided that, like our families, we were direct opposites. You were beautiful, luminescent. I was just Sam. Plain old Sam. But we were magnets, poles reaching out across a valley and coming together purely because they were unable to stay apart. And maybe it was more of me being pulled into your gravity like everybody else, but that didn't change the fact that somehow, magnets work. And somehow, so do we.

Chapter 17

Aunt Sheridan is a pack-rat. She doesn't need stuff, but she likes stuff, maybe even more than she likes cooking, so she's always showing up bogged down with stuff. On Monday, she turned up to pick me up after school with a legion of baggage in the backseat of her little car.

"I guess you went shopping," I observed, but very cautiously. Say too much to Aunt Sheridan and you end up with a never-ending story.

"Oh, I did." She turned to me, grinning, and began to tell me about her day of Christmas shopping as she drove away. She'd managed to have every family member accounted for.

"And I got this amazing set of paintbrushes for your cousin, Peter; you know, the one who paints? Well, they were on sale at Target so they were only four ninety-nine..."

Peter is my second cousin in Canada who we've never met, and who I doubt really does like painting. He's five; he likes smearing colors on the wall with his hands in a way that's cute enough for his mom to take pictures and post the masterpieces on Facebook. I told my aunt this, but she just huffed and said that we'd be encouraging his artistic talent and Sam, when that boy's got a gallery in the Louvre you'll wish you agreed.

I love my aunt. But sometimes, I don't.

"Oh and Sam," she said, stalling the car as she approached a red light, "I went to a flea market in Beaverton and got you a great sweater."

I was immediately wary, because the things that my aunt usually thinks are great are either broken or bedazzled. I held my breath as she reached into the backseat, and even though I had my hopes up that maybe I would be wrong, that sweater was everything I expected it to be and was even worse besides.

"What is that?" I demanded. The sweater was brown, but centered on it was some kind of furry, feathery, white and red creature that popped out from the simple fabric.

Aunt Sheridan stared at it. "I'm not sure. I think it's a rooster." She was still examining it when the light turned green, and cars behind her began to honk. I opened my mouth to tell her, but she continued, "But you love it, don't you?"

"Well, I mean, I—"

"You love it," she affirmed, tossing it onto my lap and simultaneously flooring the gas pedal.

Nothing was ever up to question when it came to Aunt Sheridan.

I stared at the sweater dubiously, already hearing Carson and his friends' snide comments about it in my head. Maybe, I thought, there was some way to slyly burn it while my aunt was at work. Maybe you would want it. Well, probably not—but maybe you could burn it.

As I eyed the thing, Aunt Sheridan glanced over at me, peeling her eyes from the road every few seconds to grin. When I finally turned and looked back at her, confused, her smile just grew.

"So, Sam," she sung, "when will you be asking Ellery out on a real date?"

I felt my jaw drop. That, certainly, was a question I wasn't prepared for at all. Was I even going to ask you out? I wanted to, sure. I'd thought about it. I'd also never asked a girl out before with positive results, and even though I didn't think you would blatantly reject me (Like Kayle Park in freshman year), I didn't think I'd be able to handle it if you rejected me at all.

Better safe than sorry, and all that.

"Ah, well, I wasn't really—"

"Because you're going to ask her out, right?"

"Maybe, but I don't know if—"

"Well, you want to, though, right?"

I scratched my head, blushing. "Er, yeah, I do. I just don't want her to, um, well, say no."

Aunt Sheridan laughed loudly, glancing at the sweater in my hands. "Wear that, and you'll be fine," she advised. "No girl in her right mind would turn down a boy with a rooster on his sweater."

Chapter 18

“My latest assignment for my creative writing class,” you said on Tuesday afternoon, “is to write a paragraph detailing the 'essence' of a person you know.” We were sitting on the couch in the teashop. You was a pen in one hand and a mug in the other. “And I've decided to write about you. You're welcome.”

I raised an eyebrow, hiding a smirk. “Thank...you?”

“You should be honored,” you declared, pointing your pen at me. “One day, when I'm a famous author, someone will read that paper and you'll be famous by default.”

“Oh, by default.” I rolled my eyes jokingly. “I see how it is, Ellery. It's not like I actually did anything to deserve it.”

You pursed your lips, your eyes owlish. “Well, sure you did something, Sam. You exist!”

There was a moment of silence there, as I wondered at the seriousness in your eyes and thought that maybe, maybe, you truly meant that, but then you broke it with a small smile and an elbow to my arm.

“You deserve good things, Sam,” you assured me. “Even from an evident goddess like myself.”

You were just teasing, and I knew that, so I let out a snort. But I was thinking, even though you were absolutely crazy, that wasn't so far from the truth. At least, that was the case in my eyes.

I watched you laugh at me, your head tilting back so that your hair slipped away from your face. I studied your little quirks; the way you spooled your hair around your pinky as you straightened, the shift in your features as you set down your teacup and hefted your pen and poised it over the notebook that lay on your criss-crossed legs.

"I wonder," you said thoughtfully, "how would one describe the essence of Sam?" Your gaze flicked over to me and meandered across my face as you chewed on the clicker of your pen. I saw your lips twist in speculation.

"Books," I supplied, glancing at the novel in my hand. "There definitely have to be books."

You nodded. "Books." Then the sound of ink on paper. You looked up at me. "And the color blue," you added, as an afterthought. "For your eyes."

"And tea."

"And tea," you echoed. "Peppermint tea."

I turned red, because I didn't realize you had noticed and it made me smile to know you did.

"And blushing." You smirked. "Definitely blushing." When I turned an even deeper shade of scarlet, you reached over and patted my hand, saying, "Don't worry about it. I just have that kind of effect on people."

You didn't even realize how true that was. One moment of eye contact, and I felt my stomach twist happily. Every time I saw you smile was a private treasure. All the little details were important, and I wanted to know everything that I could about you. You were quickly consuming my thoughts, and I didn't even think I minded.

"What else?" you asked, drawing me away from your face and back to reality. "Do you play sports?"

I shrugged. "Track, a few years ago. Never loved it."

"Hm." A thoughtful frown appeared on your face. "Well, then, what are you good at?"

I thought about it briefly, trying to pull some kind of talent from my uneventful life. Was there anything, really? I was coming up blank.

"Nomenclature," I proffered. "I'm good at nomenclature."

You wrinkled your nose. "I hate chemistry, so no. Try again, and this time, let's not make it school related."

Setting down my book, I tried my hardest to come up with something. I really, really did. But when all you do is read, there really isn't much else to talk about. I glanced around the room, hoping to find inspiration in one of the other customers. There was nothing, but my eyes caught on the board game cabinet on the other wall and specifically on one game that I always beat my sister at when we were kids.

"I'm really good at Candyland," I stated proudly.

You turned to look at me slowly, one eye squinted and a hand on the side of your face. "Really, Sam? That's all you've got? A game for three- to-five-year-old children?"

"What can I say?" I shrugged. "I'm young at heart."

You gave me a final snort, but I saw you write them both down in your curly, heart-dotted handwriting. Then you paused, evidently as unsure about what else there was as I was.

I sighed. "I don't think I'm good at anything that counts, Ellery." Shaking my head, I picked up my book again, then set it down, then picked it up. I guess that means I'm indecisive.

When I looked at you again, I saw a fire growing in your eyes; your irises went up in flames. But it was a brilliant, vermillion shade that I couldn't see but knew existed anyway.

"Yes you are, Sam." You sounded absolutely convinced. "Everyone is."

I scoffed. "You're good at ballet and writing. My aunt is good at cracking jokes. My uncle is a great handyman, and my sister has always been amazing at art. And what do I do? I sit in my room and read books."

There was silence for a moment as I sunk deeper into the couch to emphasize my words. You were looking down, but your eyebrows were knit and your lips were curled down and you really did look concerned.

"No, that's not true," you murmured gently. "No, you're—you know what you're good at Sam?" You sped on, not waiting for an answer. "You're good at making me smile."

I opened my mouth but you held up a hand, nodding quickly now. "It's the truth. We've known each other for what, a week? Two? But you have this—this effect on me, and I don't know what it is but I can't help but smile whenever I'm around you." You wrote the words on your paper in all capital letters: GOOD AT MAKING ME SMILE. Then you turned back to me. "I think that counts."

I didn't know what to say, because thank you seemed weak and everything else in my head was corny. And I guess you didn't either, after that, because you just pressed your lips together and reached over and touched your hand to mine. You didn't move away this time, you stayed there, and as we sat with our hands touching, shoulder to shoulder in that quiet moment, I wondered if this was the right time for me to ask you the question that Aunt Sheridan and I had been discussing the day before.

But then you tilted your head so that it rested on my shoulder, and everything in my head promptly flew out because your hair was tickling my nose and it smelled like cookies and Christmas and everything warm. And you were so beautiful, breathtakingly so, and I found myself wanting to brush the hair out of your eyes but I was frozen in place by your closeness.

I wondered then, in some halted moment of messy thought, what the essence of you would be. And I didn't think that it's be one thing, or a collection of related things, because you were so many people all at once. You had countless sides, and everything about you was a crazy, chaotic whirlwind that was laughter and warmth and happiness and at the same time, sadness and nostalgia, all rolled up into one person. One beautiful person.

Like a kaleidoscope, I thought idly. A hurricane of colors and feelings and words, twisting and reforming and being everything you possibly could in one sweep of existence. That was the essence of you, I decided. You were kaleidoscopic.

Chapter 19

I knew that you weren't perfect. I understood this, because no one is perfect and anyone who believes themselves to be so is evidently very self-centered. And you were not that person.

So I knew that you weren't completely flawless, and I loved that. I loved all your little quirks, the way you couldn't keep your bangs out of your face, the slight shade difference in the color of your eyes. Maybe you thought I didn't notice these things; maybe you wanted to keep them a secret. But even though I guess you'd fuss about them, calling them "imperfections," I thought those little things made you all the more beautiful.

It took nearly two weeks of knowing you to realize that you didn't feel the same way.

It was a Wednesday; you had another performance that night, but it wasn't until the evening and you'd taken the free time to meet me at the bookstore. It wasn't a date, not really. But I'd asked you to come and you'd agreed, and maybe you thought we were just going as friends but that didn't change your answer so I figured I'd just take it.

Somehow, we'd ended up sitting on the racetrack rug in the kid's section, a collection of Dr. Seuss beside us, reading the picture books back and forth to each other and ignoring the toddlers watching us like we'd lost our minds. And maybe we had, but we were both laughing and my stomach was beginning to hurt because of it but I was fairly certain it was the best feeling ever.

We were sitting close, shoulder to shoulder, leaning against against a bookshelf. Every now and then as you laughed, your head would touch my shoulder and I would smell that familiar collection of winter and warmth, and it was familiar and safe and made me want to draw you into my arms and never let you go.

You had finished reading Oh, the Places You'll Go!, but I didn't realize it until you said, "Earth to Sam! Is anybody home?"

I swam back into reality, because I'll admit, I'd been daydreaming. I'd been thinking—wondering—if it would be so bad to ask you out right this minute, if it would be awkward or if I would be awkward or if—well, who was I kidding; of course I would be awkward.

"I'm listening," is all that came out.

You smiled, rolling your eyes at me and then tilting your head back onto one of the shelves. Your eyes drifted shut and you pulled your legs to your chest, taking a deep breath before sighing it all out. Your eyelashes brushed against your cheeks, your pale lips were curled slightly upward, and maybe there was nothing particularly fantastic about that, but I could look away.

Until you spoke.

"Sam, stop it," you murmured, and your eyes were still closed but your lips were moving.

I blinked. "What?"

"Stop looking at me, like...that." You flung your arm in a haphazard gesture, narrowly missing my face.

"Like what? Ellery, your eyes are closed, what are you—"

"Sometimes you look at me," you mumbled, cracking open your eyelids, "and it's as if you think I'm something phenomenally special. I can feel it, and I see it in your eyes. The way you look at me is like I'm a queen, or a goddess, or someone who's extraordinary. But I'm not, Sam. I'm not." You shook your head. "You're seeing me as someone who's bigger and better than I actually am, and I don't know why that is, but it's false. I'm just a normal girl—I'm not special or stunning or whatever you think I am, and you need to understand that."

Your voice fell to a whisper, and I was shocked. It felt as though someone had pressed me against the wall with a million stickpins. I didn't understand, because when I looked at you I saw everything good and I didn't see how you couldn't see the same things.

"Ellery, why did you tell me that?" I asked softly.

You shrugged. "I—I just...I guess I knew that eventually you'd figure out that I'm nothing great, and—and I didn't want you to be disappointed." You looked down, curtaining your face with your hair and picking at your nails.

I took a deep breath, licked my lips, and sighed.

"I know," I began, "that a person isn't who they really are in one snapshot of time. I've only seen you in certain places, and I know that you'd act differently around your family, or your friends. I know that the Ellery I see in front of me—that's not you, not completely. You're so much more; you're mistakes and greatness, you're smart and weak, and I know you aren't the person I'm seeing you as right now."

I paused for breath, and when I looked at you, your eyes were wide and shining with moisture.

"But that doesn't change the fact that you're special," I continued. "Maybe you don't think that, and maybe sometimes you don't feel like that, but I swear, you are. You're every bit as beautiful, all throughout, as I think you are, and maybe I don't know you all to well, but I know that for certain." I rubbed my forehead, sighing. "I can't let you think that you're any less that you are," I said forcefully. "I just—I can't stand to think that you're going around every day with some kind of ridiculous idea that you're not amazing. Because you are, and I don't know how to prove this to you, but you're—you're everything, and you have to believe me."

For a long moment, neither of us spoke. We sat there and stared at each other in a bookstore in the middle of Portland, sitting on a playroom rug, and there was a collection of tears gathering in your eyes and as I continued to watch, a few leaked out and trickled down your cheeks. Then you sprung forward, throwing your arms around me and squeezing tightly, your face buried into my chest.

"Sam," you breathed, and that was all. Just my name, but there was so much feeling and gratitude and relief behind it that I felt my heart skip a beat. And it was only one word—but that was enough.

Chapter 20

I don't know how friendship happens, exactly; how a relation-
ship can go from strangers to acquaintances to friends without
your even realizing it. I didn't know how, since that day in the
teashop when I first saw you, we had become so inseparable.

Sometimes, when I thought about it, it all seemed too good to
be true. Sometimes, I wondered where I would be if I hadn't seen
you on that day in the teashop; if there had been an empty seat on
the day you sat next to me. I couldn't imagine it, but I guess that
was strange, because I couldn't grasp the idea of you not being in
my life and I couldn't get my head around the fact that you were.

I didn't want you to ever leave. Every time I saw you I wanted to
grab your hand and meld it with mine so that you'd stay, because
people were always leaving me and I hated feeling sorry for myself
but I just needed someone to prove to me that there was such
thing as forever.

As I watched you scribble into your notebook on Thursday afternoon, I wondered if that's why you wrote. Because words are
eternal, and even when you're gone they'll be there, and maybe
that's the reason why they meant so much to you. Through them,
you could be immortal.

Maybe that's why all writers write: because their words and sentences and phrases make them everlasting. That's how Shakespeare and Jules Verne and so many past figures are still here, even though they're not, because when you crack open their books or read the letters they combined, they come back to life.

And I wondered if that's why sometimes writers are angst-filled and tragic and the slightest bit out of touch with reality. It must be hard, always trying to outsmart time. I thought that must be the reason why, when you wrote, you didn't show the joy on your face that you say you feel. Your lips were a thin white line and there were creases on your forehead as you frowned at your pen. Every word had to be torn from your mind and cocooned the the folds of paper, and it wasn't pretty or easy but somehow it helped. It was just the price you had to pay for trying to last forever.

But you were lucky, really, in a strange kind of way. Writing drove you crazy, but it immortalized you. I knew very well that not everyone could be eternal.

"Sam?" Your concerned voice dove into my head and grabbed my thoughts, pulling them back to the surface of consciousness. I turned to you, your hand on my arm and your eyes were worried.

"What?" I mumbled.

You shifted your hand away, leaning over to pick something up off the floor. It was my book, lying open on the ground, the page lost.

"Here." You handed it to me, pressing a hand against your notebook so that it wouldn't fall. I thanked you, softly, and tried to trace my thoughts back to where I'd gotten lost. As I did, I heard you say, "Wait, here's something else. Is this yours?"

I looked up, and you were reaching for the familiar slice of a photograph that served as my bookmark. No, no, no! My stomach twisted, and I tried to grab it before you but you were closer and your fingers had closed around it by the time I'd lifted my arm.

I watched you pick it up, your features knotted in confusion, and set it on the notebook on your lap. You were silent for a moment, and I was dying to know what you were seeing and what you were thinking and praying to God that you wouldn't ask the question—

"Who are they, Sam?"

Your voice: soft and reverent, barely above a whisper. Your thumb: trailing the jaggedly scissored border of the photograph. Your eyes: turning to me, gentle, questioning.

I could see the picture in my head: the tall man with dark hair and kind brown eyes, the brunette woman with smiling irises the color of sea glass. Both of them, arms around each other, grinning at the camera, back when they were still here and the world was still simple and none of us knew anything about grief or loss.

Somehow, I managed the response. Two words. "My parents."

You nodded, very slowly, then became very still. You didn't pass the photo back to me, and I didn't ask for it. I just stared at you, staring at it, and wished again that I could read your mind.

"She has your eyes," you murmured.

"Had," I corrected, automatically.

And that's when it started—the rapid breakdown that overtakes my mind whenever I think of my parents, whenever I remember that they're past tense and not here and that they never will be again.

I was seeing it all over again, even though I hadn't been there. I'd been coming up with reenactments of it in my head, and I didn't know why I was torturing myself but it started when I was twelve and they'd told me, and even though I could cope with it better now, sometimes I just couldn't. I couldn't.

And so I lived through it all, the event I'd never witnessed. My parents on a bus, going out for their anniversary. April 14th. They were going up to Seattle for the day, but their car was being being repaired and they had to take the bus, even though Aunt Sheridan had told them never to trust public transport in the city. Aunt Sheridan. So much younger then, but still odd. That time, she had been right.

The bus driver wasn't thinking straight. That's what he told us. That's the excuse he gave for plowing his goddamn bus onto railroad tracks and into the path of an incoming freight train. That's the statement that he, as the sole survivor of the accident, gave to the court when he was tried for killing twenty innocent people.

My parents among them.

I saw the smoke in my head. The shriek of tires, the protesting cries of gears, the skidding cacophony of metal against metal. I saw the flames go up and expand, swallowing that bus and making sure that everyone who had survived the impact was gone too. And in my mind's eye, I watched the bus driver crawl from the rubble and run, run like the coward he was, a man covered in soot dashing away from a hellish horizon.

Too much. Too much. It was too much, it was a breakdown, and then my head was in my hands and I was biting down a scream and I didn't even realize I'd spoken out loud until I felt your hand on my back, warm and familiar and your voice whispering the words, "I'm so sorry."

We didn't like sorry but I guess you knew that there was nothing else to really say.

Deep breaths: three seconds in, three seconds out. Then another. And another. And one more for good luck, to stop my swimming vision, so that when I looked up I wouldn't see everything on fire.

There were no tears. The tears had been gone for years now, dried out by all that fire. But the pain was still there, and fresh, and sitting up sent a new wave of it into my chest. It wouldn't go away ever; it was my personal demon, always inside me.

You swallowed hard, your hand slipping down to mine and lacing our fingers together beneath the table. "When you said you knew what it felt like to lose someone," you breathed, "you meant it."

I nodded harshly, leaning my elbow against the wood and trying to draw air into my lungs even though there were shards of glass in my heart.

"Yeah." My voice was nearly silent. "Yeah, I did."

It was another one of those moments, the kind that doesn't need words because it explains itself. It was the kind where you forget that there are other people around because your breathing is deafening in your ears and there's a pretty girl beside you who's your friend and who's holding your hand and maybe trying to make you just as everlasting as she is.

As you are.

I wished that other people could have the forever that you do. I wished that my parents didn't have to just leave, because leaving is cruel and leaving hurts and leaving doesn't care about stabbing holes in hearts. It's even harder when the leaving isn't just leaving, but it's actually gone. Gone and never coming back. Gone forever.

My parents were gone forever, but maybe that's the sick plot twist of life. I wanted them to be eternal, and they were. It's just that they were eternal in absence, in death, and you were eternal in life. I wanted it to stop. I wanted to stop walking tightropes and stop missing them so much. I wanted to turn back time so you didn't see the picture and I didn't have a breakdown. Everything was a mess, such a mess. And I wanted relief. I just wanted something to for once, last forever.

Chapter 21

Friday was one of those rare school days, the kind where everyone is on the edge of their seats and teachers are smiling and there's a breathless, anticipatory feeling dangling in the air like mistletoe. It was always like this before break, when we could taste freedom on our tongues and the feeling was so wonderful that even the school Scrooges were smiling. Carson Myles even wished me happy holidays, and even though his exact words were, "Merry Christmas, twerp," I still returned the greeting with a smile.

I was so happy by the end of the day, and I figured that the only thing that would make it better would be to see you. But you weren't going to be at the teashop; you'd texted me the night before to say that you had a club meeting then another performance and you wouldn't have time. Pathetically, I'd gotten to the point of dependency where not seeing you for a day gave m withdrawal-like effects, and I couldn't get you out of my head until I'd seen your smile. It was beginning to worry me a little, but I guess it was just the way things are when you really, really like someone.

Maybe it was the intoxicating feeling of the holidays, or the Disney movies we'd been watching in my classes throughout the day, but I suddenly wanted to be the knight in shining armor that you obviously didn't need, the prince who would sweep you off your feet. At the very least, I wanted to show up and surprise you after school.

Aunt Sheridan let me use her car, but she did give me a funny look because even though I have my license she knows how much I hate driving. Then, when I told her that I was going to see you, she got this misty-eyed expression and smiled and told me to drive safe.

Sometimes I don't understand women.

I got lost a couple of times, because I don't know anything on the other side of the bridge too well, but eventually I made it to Franklin and then I was parked in the student parking lot wondering what the hell to do with myself. Sometimes I don't really think things through, and my sister always tells me this is because I'm guided by my emotions which is something girls are apparently supposed to like. I hoped you would like the fact that I was climbing the front steps of your school in the chilly December wind, uninvited, and had no idea where I was supposed to go. Because I was lost, so I wasn't enjoying it all too much.

I figured that my best bet was to hang around out front and try not to look too awkward, even though that was basically impossible. Thankfully, it wasn't too crowded because school had been out for a while now, and you were only still there since your community service club was making shoe boxes to send to a shelter in the city. Only a few people passed me as I sat on the brick fence in front of the school, passing time, and they didn't seem to notice me. I was virtually invisible, and sometimes that's a good thing.

It's also a good thing that I'm not invisible to you, and you couldn't possibly understand how much warmer it made me feel (it was really cold), when I heard your voice, confused as it was, calling my name.

"Sam? What are you doing here?"

Then footsteps; your shoes slapping pavement, getting louder, and when I looked up there you were, cocooned in another terrible Christmas sweater with a giant scarf wrapped around your neck. Your freckle-dusted nose was red from the cold, but you were smiling and you looked like the perfect picture of winter.

I'd had all these things to say to you, but they all slipped from my mind when I saw you standing there. "I, um, just came to say hi," I managed. "So...hi?"

You snorted. "My God, Sam, don't be so awkward." I half-smiled as you stepped forward and linked your arm with mine, shifting your bag on your shoulder. "Regardless of why, I'm glad you came."

"I can drive you home," I offered.

The wind brushed your hair away from your face. "That would be really great."

The student parking lot was around the side of the school, past the gym and the football field. It had all been empty on my way over, but now there were three kids, two guys and a girl, leaning against the outer gym wall with cigarettes between their fingertips. Their appearance, the looks on their faces, immediately set off a warning bell in my head, and it only intensified when you tensed beside me.

"Head up, Ellery," I thought I heard you murmur.

The kids looked up just as we were passing, and you straightened and raised your chin beneath their gazes. The girl smirked, ugly and shark-like, and looked you up and down with the words, "Nice sweater, dork."

I wanted to freeze, to turn on her and shout and hit her stupid friends for laughing at her comment. But you kept walking, so I forced myself to do the same. They were idiots, and they were everywhere and I had dealt with them myself. If they didn't bother you, I wouldn't let them bother me.

"Where ya going, Ellery?" one of the guys taunted. "Running away again? Didn't think you were as chicken as your little brother." He made a chicken noise, and in my peripherals I saw him flapping his arms.

You stopped. Your arm slid away from mine, but I could plainly see the way you were vibrating with anger, your cheeks turning red and your arms becoming fists. And I could relate, because I wasn't even you and I felt the same way.

"You gonna just stand there?" the guy demanded. "If you've got a problem with us, why don't you come and tell us what it is? Or does pathetic weakness just run in your family?"

We both whirled around at the same time, but I spoke first. Shouted.

"He wasn't weak," I spat, feeling my nails digging into the flesh of my palms. I was angry, so angry, because how dare that idiot insult your family when he didn't even know you, didn't know how wonderful you were.

"That right?" The boy tossed his cigarette to the ground, crushed it beneath the toe of his shoe. "Then why didn't he fight, huh? Why'd he go and take the easy way out?"

I couldn't see your face; I didn't want to. But I heard the complete fury in your voice as you snarled the bitter words, "You have no right to say that. You don't know anything."

He snorted.

This wasn't okay. You were upset, and I couldn't stand it because people like you shouldn't ever be anything but happy, and I can't tell you how much I wanted to tear that boy to shreds right then and there, wipe that hideous grin off his face. I was seeing red, and it was scaring me, but I didn't try to quell it.

I wasn't thinking properly; I can't never do anything brave when I'm thinking properly. Every sliver of holiday spirit was gone as I strode over to that boy, leaning so casually against the wall, as if he hadn't just said such an awful thing. I wasn't myself as I reached out and grabbed the collar of his shirt, pinning him to the wall. I didn't know how to fight, but I towered over him and that was enough to send a flicker of fear through his eyes.

"You worthless piece of shit," I growled, shaking him slightly. "It's pathetic trash like you that made her brother kill himself."

He tried to laugh. "Come on, man. That little queer was the pathetic one, and we both know it."

I gritted my teeth. "The only thing I know is that you don't have a brain, a heart, or a conscience. How the hell do you live with yourself?"

"Sam," I heard you say. Your voice was hazy because it was coming through a thick red cloud. Anger. That was anger. I didn't think I'd ever been so angry before. I wanted that kid—the kid whose name I still don't know—to feel the same pain that you did. I wanted him to pay for what he said.

But then you said, "Sam, let him go," and even though you still sounded angry you were calmer than me and this was what you wanted so I had to, for you. Slowly, very slowly, I uncurled my fingers from the boy's shirt. His friends had already run, and with the way he was backing away, he looked like he wanted to do the same. But he made time for one more comment, directed at you once again.

"Hey, wimp." His voice was shaky. "Maybe try fighting your own battles next time."

Then he turned, first walking away and then glancing over his shoulder and breaking into a sprint. I watched him until he disappeared around the corner of the building, and kept staring even after that, trying to calm down, until I felt your gloved hand on my arm.

When I turned to you, somehow, you were smiling.

"My hero," you declared, your eyes shining.

I scratched my head, frowning. I hadn't meant to react that way to him; I just couldn't help it.

"Who was that?" I questioned.

You toed the ground, uncomfortable. "Just some idiot. It's not a big deal, really." Then, quieter, "Happens all the time."

I wondered about that as we headed for Aunt Sheridan's car, arm in arm again. I was silent, because I didn't think there was any proper way to really respond to that. We were both silent. But I didn't understand—I just didn't. I knew bullies, and I'd grown up around them. I just didn't understand why someone like you would ever be a victim. Was I the only one who saw you for who you really were?

I opened the passenger door for you, but when I climbed into the driver's seat, I didn't start the car. It was cold, but I just sat there and let the quiet wash over us and ran my head in circles, just wondering how. And you stared at your hands.

I didn't want to ask how they knew about your brother. Or when it started. Or why. I doubted you would want to answer. Questions help nothing, I know. Sometimes silence does. Sometimes it drives you mad, or course. But often it makes everything calm.

When you broke it, your voice was soft, placid. "Thank you, Sam," you murmured. "For standing up for me. I meant what I said, about you being a hero. You're brave, and I don't think you realize that." Your hand was on my arm, but I couldn't look at you.

I shrugged, embarrassed. I didn't think you needed a hero, not really, and I didn't think I was one. You should know that no matter what you think, I'm not brave, and I'm not strong. But I can pretend that I am, for you.

Chapter 22

The year's first snowfall came on Saturday. I was woken up by a phone call at nine, which annoyed me at first because I had to reach out of my warm comforter to find my cellphone. Then I realized it was you, and I couldn't answer soon enough.

"Sam!" you cried, before I could even speak. "Sam, it's snowing outside!"

"What?" I scrambled out of bed, my legs tangling in the blankets so that I landed on my face instead of my feet. But from the floor, lying upside down, I could see the whiteness drifting down outside my window.

"Do you see it?" Your voice was crackling through the speaker, and in the background I heard the sound of you banging around in your room. "Sam, do you see it?"

"I see it!" I assured you, laughing. "I'm at my window right now, I promise." You squealed. "You know that park? The one we went to last week? Can you meet me there?"

I hesitated. "Well, it's kind of early, I—"

"Please, Sam!" you begged.

I think we both knew that I couldn't say no. With a little bit of reluctance, I agreed, but only on the condition that we'd go for Starbucks afterward.

It's never fun to walk outside while it's snowing, but this was the kind of first snow that was light and airy. I felt the ice flakes land on my face and melt against my windbreaker, so that by the time I got to the park, my hair was damp.

There were actually a lot of people out; adults with bags of last-minute Christmas shopping, kids with toboggans and color-ful mittens. The park was fully decorated, with garlands on the lampposts and colorful lights strung in the trees. Speakers, hidden throughout the park, blared Christmas carols into the air.

I found you in the midst of it all, spinning around beside a bare tree and catching snowflakes on your tongue. For a few moments, I just stood and watched you, mesmerized by the way your hair twisted in waves down your back, the blush on your cheeks, the way your pale lips were curled into a smile of private joy. I leaned against the tree until you came to a dizzy stop, hands on your knees, laughing.

"Having fun?" I asked, amused. You whirled to face me, your eyes widening and your mouth slipping into an O in a way that was so cute I almost couldn't breathe for a second.

You grinned at me, admitting, "I've never seen snow before. It's just as pretty as in the pictures." I smirked as you turned to capture a few more snowflakes on your gloved fingertips.

"Never seen snow?" I demanded, feigning disbelief. With raised eyebrows, I leaned over and picked up a handful of the stuff, packing it together in my hands. "Well, I guess that means you've never had a snowball fight?"

You shrieked as I let the snowball fly and it exploded on your shoulder. White dust sprayed your face and hair, and you stared at me with a look of shock that quickly slipped into determination.

"Oh, all right, Windermere." You whipped up a snowball of your own. "It's on."

A handful of breathy ice hit me square in the face, and I heard your waterfall laugh as I swiped it out of my eyes, already reaching for another handful. I hadn't had a good snowball fight since my sister turned sixteen and decided she was "too old," but we were both seventeen and you didn't seem any less enthusiastic than I was.

We put the little kids to shame, chasing each other through the snowy park, slipping and sliding over the icy ground and hurling snowballs at each other all the way. There was snow on my clothes and snow in your hair and snow everywhere, and it was beautiful and you were beautiful and I was certain I'd never been happier.

"All right!" You threw up your arms, released your snowballs, and flopped onto the ground. "Time out!" It had been nearly fifteen minutes of running and dodging, and we were both out of breath.

"Are you admitting defeat?" I questioned, raising an eyebrow as I sat down beside me. "Because it sure sounds like you're admitting defeat, Miss Sunshine State."

You smirked, swatting at my arm with the back of your hand. "I would never! I'm only...taking a break." You sighed and lay back in the snow. "So, what next? What else do you do in the snow?"

I shrugged. "Snow angels?"

Immediately, your face lit with surprise, and you grabbed my hand. "No!"

"N-no?"

"No way!" you shrieked. "Those exist?"

"Um." I scratched my head. "Well, yeah."

You flailed, throwing yourself spread-eagle onto the snow and waving your arms and legs like jumping jacks. It was amazing, seeing that childish joy on your face, and I couldn't help but laugh along with it. You were a bundle of happiness and ecstatic immaturity that radiated from every bit of you and washed over me and the park and turned everything magical.

I laughed as you leapt to your feet, grabbing my hands and dragging me up with you. "Look, Sam!" you cried, pointing. "Look, it's an angel!"

"I see it, I see it!"

You were another person; I'd never seen you so golden as you were in that moment, as you twirled away from me and let your thick skirt balloon around your candy cane tights. There was snow all over your clothes, but you didn't seem to care one bit.

I watched, hands in the pockets of my jeans. The snow had stopped falling, but that didn't make the winter wonderland any less exciting. Especially not for you.

You raised onto your toes, pirouetting on the icy ground, your arms lifting to form a perfect oval above your head. Hands relaxed, middle finger to thumb, chin high like a true ballerina.

But I guess turning on ice is different than on stage, because you lost your balance and tripped, squealing, right into me. I stumbled back and wrapped my arms around you to steady us both. Your hands were on my shoulders, and you were stepping on my feet but I found myself not caring because you were looking up at me and you hadn't moved away.

"T-thanks," you murmured, barely audible. I felt you link your fingers together behind my neck.

"S-sure," I breathed, staring down at you in nervous awe.

Was this happening? Were you really here, in my arms, your face inches away from mine? I was half afraid that this was some kind of cruel dream, that any minute now I would wake up and you would be gone. The idea of that was so terrifying that I pulled you even closer, my hands on the small of your back. Dream or not, I didn't want to let you go.

"Uh…" You swallowed, your green-eyed focus shifting away from my eyes, down my nose, and finally pausing at my lips.

What was it that my sister had told me? When a girl stares at your lips, she wants you to kiss her. I didn't know if you wanted me to kiss you, but I wanted to kiss you. Any number of things could happen after, but this was right now, and right now, your face was so close to mine that there was really no question about what I had to do. For once in my life, I had to take a chance.

Don't think, don't think, I thought as I pressed my lips to yours.

I'd never kissed a girl before. Never ever in my nearly-eighteen years of life. But I was kissing you, and you were kissing me back, and it was so perfect and natural that it was if we were meant for each other. I hoped that was the case, because your lips were so soft and you were so beautiful and if this was real there was evidently something right in the world. Something wonderful.

It felt like a century; it was probably ten seconds. Maybe that's a sign of a good kiss, when you lose all proper perception of time because you're so utterly lost in the moment. I think it was also a good sign that when we broke apart, you were smiling. Our noses touched, and your cheeks were bright red, and I was anxious and wonderstruck but when I tried to pull away, you stopped me.

"Stop right there," you ordered lightly. "I'm not done." You lifted your chin and closed your eyes, leaning closer again. There was snow on your eyelashes, little white flecks that shimmered under my gaze. Your smiling lips were right there, in front of me, so close that it was dizzying. And well—what could I do, really, in that moment, but take a chance...and kiss you again?

Chapter 23

I couldn't stop smiling.

When I walked home on Saturday, I was smiling. As I went out to do my Christmas shopping, I was smiling. When I went to sleep, I was smiling.

On Sunday morning, I woke up smiling.

I guess that's just the way it is, when you find out that the person you like feels the same way. It's a mix of butterfly nervousness and diamond excitement and a giddy anticipation that crawls out of your stomach to mercilessly tickle your heart. And while it sounds uncomfortable, it's actually a breathtaking feeling, and I wonder if maybe it's how all those bands in the sixties felt when they were writing those crazy songs, except, y'know, that was drug-induced and this was completely natural.

My aunt and uncle noticed, of course. They don't always pay much too attention to me, but I guess it's hard not to notice when someone who lives in your house is grinning uncontrollably. It wasn't helping that every time I tried to be serious, I'd think of you and my lips would stretch out again without any consent from my brain whatsoever.

It was hopeless, really.

Breakfast was an excruciating interrogation, as my aunt reached a new level of multitasking by bombarding me with questions while simultaneously burning a batch of French toast. Uncle Dill snorted and sipped coffee through it all, and I did my best to focus on completing a Sudoku puzzle in the newspaper which, in all honesty, I had no idea how to do. I figured that if Aunt Sheridan's food was too disgusting, I could sustain myself by eating the newsprint.

As a last resort.

"It's Ellery, isn't it?" Aunt Sheridan prodded, waving a spatula in my direction. "Isn't it, Sam? Is she finally your girlfriend?"

I replied with a messy mumble, because I really didn't know the answer to the question myself. I had no idea where the line between friend and girlfriend was drawn, and even though I figured kissing was a good point for it to turn over, I was pretty sure that there had to be some formal Facebook status-changing or something in order to make it completely official.

Eventually, I guess Aunt Sheridan realized that she wouldn't be getting a straight answer anytime soon, so she banished me to the living room to wrap my cousins' presents. I didn't want to wrap presents, I wanted to see you. I wanted to pull you close and kiss you in the snow, and most of all I wanted you to stay in my life forever because I suddenly wasn't sure how I'd ever be able to manage without you.

Not that you were gone; it's just that you had church in the morning and family time in the afternoon and a final Nutcracker performance in the evening, which really left no time to spend with maybe-boyfriends in the midst of it.

It was really hurting my head, trying to figure out where we stood now. But I had to wrap presents, and I thought that might help take my mind off it.

"And while you're at it," added Aunt Sheridan, "call your sister, would you? She still hasn't said whether or not she's coming up for Christmas."

I mumbled something about how there was a phone right there, do it yourself why don't you, but I really didn't mind calling my older sister. Since she moved down to California for college two years ago, I'd only been seeing her about three times a year, and lately she'd even been "too busy" for her usual weekly calls. She was a dope so I'd never admit it, but I really did miss her sometimes.

I dialed while collecting our assorted medley of wrapping paper and tried to gather them all in one hand as the phone rung. There was soon a click of answering, but the first thing I heard was a yawn, and my sister's voice didn't come through till I'd dumped the rolls onto the couch.

"What?" she snapped. Typical response when she's woken up.

"Ashley, it's Sam," I replied, unfazed.

"I know it's Sam, you turd, I have caller ID." There was the creak of springs, another yawn. "Why the hell are you calling this early?"

It was ten A.M. I told her so. She snorted.

"Exactly. Way too early."

I could imagine her sitting there, pulling at her blonde hair with her face twisted up like it used to on Christmas mornings when we were little I'd run into her room and scream purely for the sake of being obnoxious. She'd had a Nerf gun under her bed, and she'd chase me out with it, shooting all the while.

But that's when we were little, and things were different now.

Ashley sighed. "So...wanna tell me why you called? It'd better be important."

I was about to answer when another voice materialized through the speaker at my ear: a tired male voice that mumbled the words, "Who is it, babe?"

My sister responded calmly: "Just my little brother; go back to sleep." There was the sloppy sound of a kiss, then a rustling and creak of floorboards as my sister stood up. I'd never seen her apartment, but I could see her shuffling out of the room, arms crossed, to take my call somewhere else.

"Ash," I said slowly, "who was that?"

Pause. Then, "No one, Sam. It doesn't matter."

My eyes darted around and I ducked in front of the couch, though I doubted my aunt and uncle were within hearing distance or cared enough to listen. "It absolutely matters if there's some random guy in your bed," I hissed. "What the hell are you doing with yourself now?"

There was another beat of silence, but this one was longer and this time, there was a sharp intake of breath from her end of the line. I knew immediately that I'd crossed some boundary, but it was too late to pull my words back.

"I'm living my life is what I'm doing with myself, Sam," she sneered, louder than I expected. "In case you've forgotten, you're my younger brother. I'm twenty years old and perfectly capable of doing whatever I want, thank you very much." She scoffed. "Oh, and by the way, he's not 'some random guy', he's my boyfriend."

I didn't know she had a boyfriend. The last time I'd talked to her was over a month ago, and I thought she would have called to tell us. She always used to tell us big news before. I wasn't sure what had changed.

"Oh." I licked my lips. "Well, sorry."

"Whatever."

I didn't think I knew who my sister was anymore, but I wanted to pretend that she was still the same Ashley who had left for college two years ago. So I just glossed over that final spat word with a quiet cough and tried to steer back to the original conversation.

I asked her if she was coming up for Christmas, and at first all I got was silence. I worried for a moment because I thought maybe she'd been angry enough to hang up, but then she sighed again and haltingly explained that no, she wouldn't be visiting, because one of her friends was throwing a big Christmas party and she and her boyfriend (his name was Nick) were planning to go.

"Are you kidding me?" I demanded. "Ashley, come on! You've never missed a Christmas before."

"Yeah, well, there's a first time for everything, I guess."

I groaned. "Are you sure there's no way you can make it? Do you have to go to the party?"

Ashley sighed, but this time, it was different. This sigh wasn't a "God, Sam, you're such an idiot" kind of sigh, it was a "you don't understand the adult world, oh naïve little brother" kind of sigh, and it was so condescending that it took the place of any words she could have said.

It was betrayal, in some kind of strange form. I guess really, it was just my sister growing up and moving on with her life, and I should have been happy for her but I wasn't, I really wasn't, because I was part of her life too and I wanted proof that I meant more to her than some stupid frat party. It was incredibly selfish of me, but she was my older sister and I had to try to convince her to come.

"Please, Ashley?" I begged. "We all miss you, and we have your presents, and Aunt Sheridan isn't cooking so the food will be good, and I really wanted you to come up so you could meet my—"

My—

"Your what, Sam?" asked Ashley, sounding very sick of talking to me.

My girlfriend, Ellery, I wanted to say, but that didn't sound right to describe you. My friend, Ellery. But that wasn't quite right either. I even contemplated this really cool girl I know, but then I realized something that jumped out of the silence on the other side and bit me right in the nose: Ashley didn't care.

She could pretend—she would pretend—but the kind of quiet she was hitting me with wasn't anticipatory or interested. It was just bored, tired. Uncaring. I didn't know when she had stopped, but I guess the days of her listening to me were over. And I decided not to tell her about you, because the idea of her not caring hurt even more than the fact that she wasn't going to visit.

"No one," I mumbled. "Never mind."

She sniffed. She didn't pry. "Okay. Well…if that's all, I should probably go. I'll talk to you later, and maybe I can visit in January or something. For your birthday."

She wasn't going to visit; I knew as well as she did. But I pretended I didn't. "Yeah, that'd be awesome," I said, feigning enthusiasm. "We'll see." I picked at the wrapping paper in front of me. "I love you, Ash. Merry Christmas."

Again, she paused, and again, she sighed. "Love you too, twit-face. Bye."

She hung up.

Love, because we're siblings and love is obligated. Of course she loved me. But I think if I'd said "like," she wouldn't have used the same response, because at that point, I didn't think my sister liked me much at all.

I wasn't smiling anymore.

I went to the kitchen to tell my aunt what my sister had said, and she said "what a shame" without even looking away from the dishes she was washing. I sat down at the table again, across from my uncle, who looked up and peered at my aunt through his reading glasses.

"Guess that means we can go to Jon's party, doesn't it?" he remarked.

Aunt Sheridan heaved a dramatic breath. "Jon's house smells, his food is stale, and his wife is even fatter and crabbier than you. The only reason you want to go is because he hoards beer in his basement." She didn't turn around, but she paused and shrugged. "But whatever you want, you're the dictator."

I'm not sure those two like each other, either.

"You know Jon, right, Sam?" Aunt Sheridan questioned. "Do you want to come along?"

I blinked. "You're going to a party? But we always have dinner together, just the four of us."

"I know, sweetie, but since your sister's not visiting, it'd be nice to do something different, don't you think?"

No. No, I didn't think so at all. But Aunt Sheridan obviously did, so I just smiled and agreed but said that no, I'd just stay home because I really didn't like Jon and he had a one-eyed cat that gave me the creeps. Except I didn't say that last part.

"I can't believe she's not coming," I mumbled, pressing my temples as my aunt turned off the sink and shed her rubber gloves. She turned and smiled at me, sympathetic.

"Don't worry yourself too much, Sam," she said. "You know Ashley's always been a stubborn old mule."

Of course I knew that. She'd always been stubborn and snappy, quick to form opinions but even quicker to hold her ground. I'd always admired her for that, because I've never been good at standing up for myself. In some ways, her strength reminded me of you, although of course you were very different in pretty much every other aspect. For instance, I thought, smiling a bit, unlike Ashley and my aunt and uncle and practically everyone else I knew, I had real and solid proof that you actually liked me.

And that made me smile again.

Chapter 24

When I look at people I know, I tend not to see them as they actually are. There's always their outward appearance, but there's also a swirl of color, a surge of emotion, and even strains of music in the back of my mind. Every person is a patchwork quilt of rainbow hues and pictures cut from vibrant memories, and even though it's all in my head, it feels real to me.

When I look at you, I see a manila parchment wrapping all around you. It's blank at first; then you start to speak, to live, and it fills with words that snake across its surface. Stars appear, and they weave their way into your hair and under your eyelids because you're the center of their universe, and when you smile there's a burst of iridescent lavender and the memory of your lips against mine.

You are not stagnant; in my mind, you are fleeting and endless and ever-changing, and everything I feel for you, all the affection and appreciation and love, whatever kind of love it is, sends moonbeams bursting out of you. Not sunbeams, because the sun is obvious and you aren't, you're quiet and elusive like the moon, but when you're in the perfect place, you shine.

I wish I was an artist, because then I could paint you the picture of you. But even then, I don't know if I'd be able to capture you in all of your chaotic beauty. I wish I was a writer, so I could use words like you do to describe it. I wish I could make you understand how incredible you are.

I wished, on that Monday, as I watched you write in the teashop, that I could just explain the way I felt about you and the way you made me feel.

We didn't talk as much as usual, but not in a bad way. You were writing and I was reading, but every once in a while we'd both look up and our eyes would meet and we'd both smile, shyly, before looking away again. Neither of us said anything about Saturday, but I could tell from your pink cheeks that you were thinking about it as much as I was. But we didn't want to ask the looming question: where are we now?

Instead, we talked about Christmas, only one day away, and you told me how it was your favorite holiday and you absolutely couldn't wait, especially because this was going to be a white Christmas, just like in the songs. You asked me what my plans were, and when I mumbled something about staying home alone, you were appalled.

"Alone on Christmas?" you demanded, and promptly asked (well, insisted), that I go to your family's house for their annual Christmas party. Your aunts and uncles and cousins and grandparents were flying out from all over the country plus Canada, which you probably thought would persuade me, but it actually kind of worried me more than a little bit.

"I wouldn't want to intrude," I said, nervous as usual.

You snorted. "Intrude? Please, if anyone's gonna be intruding, it'll be my Uncle Clinton. He eats half the ham by himself and takes up two seats at the table."

When all I managed was a halfhearted laugh, you reached across the table and linked my fingers with yours.

"Please, Sam?" you begged, tugging my hand. "You won't be out of place or anything! I mean, Ed and Evan are bringing their girlfriends, and Emma's boyfriend is stopping by too. You have to come."

I paused. I tilted my head and looked at you and thought about that for a moment.

"What does that make me then?" I asked slowly, finally. "What does that make us?"

You considered that. I watched your lips twist and your eyebrows move together as you said, very quietly, that you didn't know. I didn't know either, and for a moment, we said nothing.

Then: "I'll go," I said, surprising myself. You looked up me with exclamation points in your eyes, and I smiled. "It'd be fun to spend Christmas with you."

You grinned at me as we sat there, holding hands across the table, and we didn't know what we were or where we stood or where we were going, but that was okay. Because then you looked at me, smirking, and said, "You know, I always said that my first boyfriend would have blue eyes."

Chapter 25

They've always told us that Christmas is about more than just boxes under a tree, and I think that's very true. Once I started growing up, I realized that gifts didn't matter to me so much, because Christmas was a time when everyone smiled and got along, even if only for a few hours.

Waking up on Christmas morning wasn't as exciting as it used to be, when I was still small enough to get away with screaming loud enough to wake the whole building, but there was still that invisible feeling in the air of everything being magical.

Aunt Sheridan and Uncle Dill and I opened presents around lunchtime, because it was our family tradition to sleep in really late on Christmas. There weren't many gifts with just the three of us, but that didn't matter because I still got to see the glee on my aunt's face as she opened the dictionary-sized cookbook I bought for her.

"Oh God, this will only encourage her," Uncle Dill muttered, but he was quickly appeased when he opened the Fleetwood Mac coffee mug I'd gotten him.

The two of them got me an old-fashioned Polaroid camera and a giftcard to the bookstore, which surprised me because I guess they knew me better than I thought. Uncle Dill got his wife a gaudy ruby ring that was just her style, and she gave him tickets to the next Ducks game. They even kissed, which doesn't happen very often, but I guess it was special because it was Christmas.

That was the morning—it was just the beginning.

All the parties started at four, when it was just starting to get dark. My aunt and uncle dropped me off in front of your house with your present and a big poinsettia plant for your parents. I wasn't sure what to expect, because I'd never been inside your house and I didn't know your family, but everyone was lovely.

Your mom opened the door and squealed over the plant, hugging me as she ushered me through the door. Your living room, clean and big and elegant, was full of dozens of unfamiliar faces, so many adults and kids and teens that my head began to spin, and I just wanted to turn and bolt out the door.

But then I saw you. You, in a red dress and thick tights, standing by the Christmas tree with an elf hat on your head. When you saw me, you beamed and danced over, twirling into my arms to the beat of the holiday song playing on the radio.

"Hey," I murmured, breathless at your smile.

"Hey," you replied. Then, quietly, you said, "I decided."

I didn't know what you meant at first, and I didn't have time to ask because you moved out of my arms and took my hand.

"Come meet everyone," you beckoned.

It was a whirlwind of names and faces as you introduced me to your grandmother, Marcia, your aunt Elsie, your five-year-old cousin Ben, and everyone in between. And quickly, I realized what you meant, because to each person you said, "This is my boyfriend, Sam."

Boyfriend. I decided I liked it.

Your aunts tried to ask me a lot of questions and some of your older cousins looked at me funny, but it really wasn't hard to smile and say hello, and soon I'd met everyone and we were back where we'd started. We stood together by the twinkling red and gold décor of your Christmas tree and watched the swirl of sweaters and wine glasses.

You got shy all of a sudden, started tucking your hair behind your ear and fidgeting. Our hands were still entwined, and I don't think either of us had any intention of letting go. I looked down at you, chewing on my bottom lip.

"You don't mind, do you?" you asked, peering up through your eyelashes.

I shook my head, taking your other hand and saying that I didn't mind at all. In fact, my head was spinning with dizzy happiness because I was still having doubts as to whether or not it was all real. You closed your eyes and sighed, softly, in a relieved kind of way that made me want to kiss you, but I didn't get the chance because your mom called everyone in to get food.

It was a formal dinner in your huge dining room, and we ended up stuck at the kids' table because your cousins claimed the last adult seats. I didn't mind, because kids are much easier to talk to than grown-ups, even though they pulled me in a dozen different directions. You laughed at me as I tried to keep up with all the conversations and I held your hand under the table.

The little ones all wanted to open presents as soon as dinner ended, and we followed behind them and all the stuffed, drunk adults. I told your mom that the food was great (it was), and she just siphoned out a bubbly laugh.

Really, I wasn't expecting you to get me anything for Christmas, and I didn't mind whether you did or not. It'd taken me long enough to decide whether or not it would be weird to get you a gift, but I ended up being glad I did, because the first thing you did when we sat down on the carpet was fish out a box from beneath the tree and toss it at me.

"For you," you said with a giant grin.

The wrapping paper had reindeer on it. There was a stick-on bow on the top, which I took off and put on top of your head. You laughed, leaning into my shoulder, but didn't take it off.

"Sam, stooop," you whined. "Open it!"

"I am," I chuckled, elbowing you lightly. I undid the wrapping paper carefully, lifted the top off the box. Inside was a book, a complete collection of Edgar Allen Poe's poems and short stories, and I was shocked because I certainly didn't expect you to remember that I liked his writing.

I opened my mouth to thank you, but you held out a hand and said, "Not yet. Look inside."

I pulled open the front cover, and out slipped a thick brown envelope with a few words scrawled across the it in your familiar handwriting.

For Sam. I wrote about us.

It was your notebook. Or one of them, at least, because I'm sure you had several. This one was smaller, and blue, and bulging with extra paper that you'd stuffed into the back. The pages were curling under the weight of the ink, because every page was brimming with words in black, in blue, in purple and green and red. You'd written me a rainbow.

"Ellery," I murmured, because I was in awe, "what—how—"

You smiled, looking down. "I wrote about us. The adventures we've had, and the ones we'll have later on. I started it the day I first saw you, and I've been writing it ever since. I—I thought it'd be perfect."

"It is," I said, running my fingers over the letter-stained pages. "It really is."

It was. It was so perfect that I was almost afraid to give you the gift I'd gotten you, because I didn't think it was nearly as amazing. But I did anyway, nervously, blushing as I slipped it in your hands.

I'd wrapped it in a map of the world, because you'd once told me that you wanted to travel the globe, and you gasped at the paper alone. You said you didn't want to open it at first, but eventually your curiosity won, and you meticulously pulled apart the wrapping.

A collection of Shakespeare's sonnets. If you could remember my favorite writer, I could remember yours.

A pen; one of the glossy ones. And a new, thick notebook with a note on the very first page.

For all your adventures to come. -Sam

I watched your lips move, reading the words, watched them curl into a smile that shimmered under the Christmas lights. You turned to me and didn't say anything, just threw your arms around me and pressed your face into my shoulder. I held you close, and for a little while all your family disappeared, the party and music and noise faded away, and it was just you and me sitting on your carpet, lost in each others' arms.

There was karaoke. There was dancing. There was a family charades game in which you tried to imitate some character from Mean Girls and everyone thought you were Spiderman. Your family was fun, and I couldn't stop smiling. This was Christmas, I thought. Not food and gifts and carols, but just being around wonderful people and feeling all the glittering emotions of the season.

By nine o'clock, things had slowed down, and we were crammed into a large recliner chair with cups of hot chocolate, watching your parents attempt to sing "Total Eclipse of the Heart." You were leaning against me, curled against my side, and I had my arm around you without caring that your entire family was watching.

"They really like you, you know," you informed me with a yawn.

I smiled down at you. "Yeah?"

"Yeah." A sleepy nod. "And they're not the only ones."

That made my heart speed up, and you intertwined our hands with gentle grace. Your heavy lids lifted, your gaze focusing above my head—and slowly, your eyes widened.

"Sam," you breathed. Your green eyes were wonderstruck, and I followed your focused up, up, up, above us.

There was a string hanging from the ceiling, and it was coiled around something green and thin and familiar.

Oh. Oh.

Mistletoe.

I looked down. Our noses were touching. I was progressively nervous, because everyone was here and what would they think and oh god what if your brother killed me?

You put a hand on the side of my face. The mistletoe twirled above our heads. The ribbon bow, still on your head, slipped to the side.

And I kissed you.

It was short and sweet; precarious and drifting. You smiled against my lips, and I drew back just slightly to tuck a strand of hair behind your ear.

"Merry Christmas, Sam," you murmured, your eyes half-closed.

I smiled, because everything was aligned under the twinkling lights. "Merry Christmas, Ellery."

I decided then that I really liked Christmas.

And mistletoe.

Chapter 26

On Thursday I took you on a proper date, because I figured since I was your boyfriend now, that was something I should do. I borrowed my aunt's car and showed up at your house, surprising you. You were fretting because you had no makeup on and were wearing an old sweater, but I told you not to change because you still looked beautiful. That made you smile, so I figured it was the right thing to say.

You kept asking where we were going, but I said nothing and that was partially because the streets were still snowy and I was somewhat terrified of careening off the road. But it was ice-skating, outdoors, and when you saw the rink you fell sideways and grabbed my arm, squealing.

"I've never been ice-skating before," you admitted, as we sat on the splintery wooden benches and I laced your skates for you.

"It's okay," I told you, taking your hand as we approached the gate on quivering legs. "You'll do fine."

I was wrong, but it was okay.

I've always been fairly stable on the ice, but you're even less coordinated in skates than you are in your regular shoes. I held both your hands and moved backwards, slowly, tugging you along as you skidded and tilted, your cheeks pink. We made it around the ring once, with all the little kids giving us strange looks as they sped past us. I didn't mind. I'd much rather stay slow with you than speed along with everybody else

"I don't think I'm very good at this, Sam," you admitted after our first lap.

I shook my head, smirking. "Nah, you're a natural."

You gave me a look. "I hear your sarcasm, Windermere."

I just linked our arms and started skating again.

You fell only once, but in a big dramatic way and with a silver bell shriek. I'd only let go of you for a second, but that was enough to send your legs flying our from under you, your arms windmilling as you landed on the white ground.

Once I was sure you were okay, I started laughing and couldn't stop, because you were parked on the ice with your bottom lip sticking out and your arms crossed over your sweater. We must have been a sight, with you throwing ice flakes at my pants and me clinging to the wall, laughing. Trying to help you up was a mistake, because you purposely pulled me down, tangling our legs and sending me sprawling onto the ice.

"All right, I'm sorry!" I cried, as you giggled and sprinkled ice into my hair.

It took another short eternity to get ourselves up, because we were both laughing so hard that our sides hurt and there were tears and our eyes and ice all over our pants. After that we decided that we'd had enough of skating for the day, so we turned in our skates to a pimply teen attendant and took to the city streets, fingers entwined.

The snow was dirty by now, but it was still snow and a big pile of it fell onto your head from a lamppost as we waited to cross the street. It all caught in your hair and glittered like a million tiny stars. You didn't try to brush it off, and as you twirled down the sidewalk with lights tangled in your auburn locks, I was glad of that.

I'd brought my new camera with me, the little Polaroid, and I took pictures of you as we walked. The snow in your hair, balanced on the precipices of your eyelashes, all captured on glossy paper squares. The dimple on your cheek that appeared as you spoke, the way you looked at me through eyes half closed. I was no photographer, but I wanted to snapshot every moment of you.

We came across a street artist in the Pearl District, a gangly beatnik wannabe who sketched portraits for six dollars. He waved at us, and you thought it'd be cute to get our picture drawn so we went over and sat on the bus stop bench he was set up around.

"Five minutes, tops," he told us, as I paid him and he began to draw. I couldn't see his eyes behind his dark glasses, but I felt the needles of his gaze on my face. I stole glances at you every few seconds, and the whisper of your smile overpowered the artist's scratching pencil and the chatter from the streets. No makeup, snowy hair, fraying sweater, but I thought you were incredible. I wondered if that meant I was in love.

The finished product was a rough sketch of our smiling faces, but the detail was stunning. Everything was accounted for, all the way down to the snowflakes in your hair. I saw you staring at the image of yourself yourself, wide-eyed, as if you couldn't believe the beautiful girl in the drawing was you. As we walked away, you asked me, in a whisper, "Is that girl really supposed to be me?"

Our fingers were linked, and your other hand held the thick paper of the sketch. I leaned into your shoulder to look at it.

Of course I didn't think it quite captured your true beauty, but it came pretty close. The only thing missing was all the life in you; something that pencils and shading couldn't catch, because it went beyond the confines of appearance and a two-dimensional smile.

"It's definitely you," I affirmed. "Why?"

You paused on the frozen sidewalk, a comma in the middle of an icy sentence. You moved your mouth like you were trying to pull the words out of the air.

"Because...because she's pretty."

I just stared at you, because I thought we'd been over this. I thought I'd told you how pretty you were, but when I looked at your expression I realized that you still didn't believe it. I didn't understand, but I grabbed both of your arms, gently, and turned you to face me.

"That's why she's you," I murmured, and then I kissed you, in the middle of the dirty snow sidewalk, because that just seemed like the only right thing to do.

When I dropped you off that evening, I made you keep the picture, the sketch of the awkward boy and, more importantly, the pretty girl with stars in her hair. You looked at me oddly when I insisted, but you didn't get it. I just wanted you to have something besides my feeble words to remind you of how beautiful you are.

Chapter 27

I took you to the record store on Burnside on Thursday evening, because you told me you hadn't gotten new music since moving to Portland. I didn't go often, but it was close—a few blocks from the bookstore.

The ceiling was dirty but the selection was good, and you squeezed my hand happily when you saw how many CDs there were. Rows and rows, rock and pop and country and R&B and everything in between. The guy at the counter, who sported the typical tattoos and multiple piercings that young Oregonians are famous for, laughed as you dashed into the fray.

"Girlfriend?" he asked me, watching you. I nodded, and he remarked, "Seems cool."

"She's really cool," I agreed.

I followed after you, dragging the soles of my shoes across the coarse carpet. Somehow, you'd already acquired a stack of at least seven disks, balanced in a stack beneath your chin. I offered to take a few, but you didn't respond because at that moment, you discovered the vinyl department.

"Sam," you said softly, freeing a hand and grabbing my arm. "What is that?"

I trailed your gaze. "The record section."

"Oh my God."

You set your CDs down on one of the racks and drifted toward the adjoining room on floating feet. I shuffled after, passing hippies young and old as you dragged your hand over the tops of the records with a reverent smile. I knew next to nothing about records, but you obviously did, and I was content to just watch you flit from bin to bin, gathering another pile.

You were wearing my jacket; I'd given it to you on our walk over, because you'd left your own at home. I wondered if you were like my sister, who never brought a jacket when she went out with a boy—not even when it was snowing or pouring rain.

It was a U of Oregon sweatshirt, and it swallowed you whole as you made your way toward me with records clutched to your chest. There was a turntable on a table by the door, and you asked the guy at the nearby counter if you could use it.

"Sure," he said, "lemme just—" But you were already moving, lifting the glass top of the turntable and setting it aside. You removed a record from the tilting stack and slid it out of its cover, then shook it from the thin paper sheath.

The guy from the counter hovered.

"Are you sure you know what you're doing?" he asked, and I was wondering the same thing.

"Of course," you replied, carefully setting the record onto the turntable. "My mom has one of these, I use it all the time."

Your fingers were careful as you raised the needle and started up the player, but when you lowered the lever you closed your eyes and placed it down at random.

"I've never heard any of these," you admitted, grabbing a pair of headphones. "I just grabbed everything that caught my eye."

I just chuckled and shook my head, because I wasn't surprised.

You lowered the headphones over your ears and I picked up the record cover, taking in the watercolor design. Passenger. I'd never heard of him, and I guess, neither had you.

But the moment the song settled into your ears, you grabbed my arm. I turned, and you were wide-eyed, your free hand pressed to one side of your face. You felt on the table for the second pair of headphones and shoved them into my chest.

"Ellery, what are you—"

"Be quiet and listen to the song," you ordered, your voice too loud because it was fighting with the volume of the music. When I hesitated, you shook my wrist. "Sam. Put on the headphones, and listen to the song."

Shrugging, I did as you said.

It was a careful melody, quiet strums and a hesitant tempo. The guy's voice was careful too, his words leaving his lips with thorough consideration, each one a gift handed over rifts of sound.

I peeked at the track list, counted how many tracks you had skipped on the record. Feather on the Clyde, it was called. I thought it sounded like feathers, soft and drifting and lovely. It sounded like the wind in summertime, like the turning pages of a good book, like your smile. When I looked at you, I knew that you heard the music too, really heard it, because your green eyes were saucers as they met mine.

I held out my hand without thinking about it. You looked at it, then placed your fingers over my palm. The song washed over us and I twirled you into my chest, wrapping my arms around you as you linked your fingers behind my neck.

You buried your face in my sweater. I pressed my cheek against your hair and closed my eyes, and we swayed along without any concern for the hipsters who kept glancing our way. When I was with you, it sometimes felt as if everything simply ceased to exist except for the two of us, wandering our own private stretch of universe and managing to transcend time itself.

Because in that moment, we were all there was. Forget the stained ceiling and the scruffy carpet. Forget the rain outside and the quickly melting snow. Forget everything else but remember us, us and the feathery music, weaving together into a single, glorious existence.

Chapter 28

We were suddenly together all the time. Every possible moment saw not just you, or me, but us, the two of us. We were synonymous, and the act of togetherness was just as wondrously natural as breathing.

I never expected someone like you to ever happen to me. When I first saw you, I didn't think that one day, we'd be spending a Friday evening blasting music in my living room, with you writing and me reading the stories you'd spun for me. Yet there we were, lit by the lambent glow of the remaining Christmas lights.

You were using your netbook, and the keys clicked quietly beneath your fingertips. Though the back of the computer was facing me, I could imagine your pink painted nails ghosting over the keyboard. The letters were faded from too much typing, and some keys held the smudgy remains of fingerprints. It was just another mark you'd left on another little thing.

In the darkened hallway, the bluish light of the TV screen in my aunt and uncle's room sent flickering streaks onto the walls. It spilled out into the living room, too, and drifted over your careful handwriting on the lined notebook pages.

Reading your journal had given me yet another reason to be amazed by you, because I realized more with every page that you really could write. Your writing went deeper than paragraphs or sentences or even words—every letter was a treasure, and I didn't know how you managed it but you did, and it was powerful.

You'd smile at me every now and then over the tops of your knees, blushing, and I knew that sharing the words on these pages was hard for you, almost too hard. But you'd done it anyway, you'd taken leaps like I had taken leaps, except your leap caught air and now you were soaring.

We didn't talk much that day; we didn't have too. The words were there in front of us, and all we had to do was breath to catch a taste of them. They were on paper, onscreen, but they were also in our minds and in the air. I watched you pluck them lithely from the sky with a simple smile or narrowed eye. The magic of your discoveries reflected onto your features, making them shine.

I sat on one side of the couch and you occupied the other, with endless tightropes of words stretched out between us. But they were not partitions, they were swirling bridges of ink and emotion, and we swung across them like they were monkey bars in a playground. They were soundless, and this was all the better because it left us with incredible space. A word in silence has even more strength than a word in sound, because the blankness leaves so much room for dauntless interpretation.

And even though I loved it when we spoke, our words in silence lit the house and brought the ceiling sagging down to join us. I'd never felt more powerful than I did in those simple moments on that simple day, when our eyes would meet and you would smile, just for a moment, before we both returned to our words. Mine, written. Yours, waiting to be written.

A simple thought: sometimes, the written word carries more life than the spoken word.

A simple truth: often, it is the simplest thoughts that are the most invincible.

Chapter 29

There are some days when the only thing that feels right is just driving around aimlessly, endlessly, knowing nothing except that you have a full tank of gas to waste and hours of time to kill. Saturday was one of those days.

So maybe I don't like driving. So maybe I'm paranoid of being behind the wheel. So to hell with maybes, it had to be done.

I picked you up in my uncle's car, a convertible, and we scouted the city streets with the top down and the radio blasting. For once, we were those annoying teenagers playing music so loud that the car pulsed. We were coasting through suburbs and bustling avenues with the wind in our eyes and our hearts in our throats.

At some point before noon, when the sky was dusty and the air was cold, Total Eclipse of the Heart began to play. We were in Beaverton, a quiet part of town, but that didn't stop you from unbuckling your seatbelt and kneeling on the passenger seat and throwing up your arms and belting along to every single word.

"Ellery," I panicked, "my God, sit down! You're gonna fall out the window or hit the windshield or—"

You turned to me as Bonnie Tyler's voice gave way to music, your hands on your hips and your bottom lip jutting out.

"Sam," you scolded, "come on. Live a little!"

I blinked at you out of the corner of my eye. "But I'm driving!"

"So? There's no law that says you can't sing while driving!"

"Uh, maybe not, but there is one that says you can't randomly unbuckle your seatbelt in the middle of the freaking—"

I didn't get to finish my sentence, because you suddenly threw your arms into the air and screamed out lyrics with more enthusiasm than I'd ever seen. You couldn't sing, but that didn't faze you.

"Ellery," I began, still nervous about your precarious perch on the seat.

"Turn around, bright eyes!" you shrieked in response.

"Can you please just—"

"Every now and then I fall apart!"

"Ellery—"

"Jesus, Sam, either sing the along with me or shut hell up!"

You were on a roll, singing in the middle of a suburban street, dizzy from the energy of that little rebellion, and I knew that there was no stopping you. You were a powder keg, a fire hazard, shooting off sparks onto the asphalt. You were unbeatable in those four minutes and thirty seconds.

It was a lost cause, trying to control your energy. I really didn't think I wanted to, not when it was so beautifully contagious. And anyway, that song really was catchy...

"Where are we?" you asked me, your hair catching the wind as you stuck your head out the window.

"Not sure," I replied calmly, staring out the windshield.

It probably should have scared me, the not knowing. But it didn't. It felt more like freedom; complete, total freedom that was addictive and intoxicating and wild.

I let the car roll to a stop. We were on some hill in a residential area that was full of trees. Actually, the entire state is full of trees, but there were a lot up here. Big trees; trees in reds and golds and oranges who still hadn't lost all their leaves.

You popped open the passenger door and stepped out onto the gravelly road, your rain boots crushing pebbles. I followed suit, and for a moment we just stood there breathing in the cold air, the kind that stings your lungs but makes everything crisper.

Then: "Hey," you said suddenly, pointing across the hood of the car. "Hey, are those—are those sheep?"

I followed your gaze, your extended finger. At first, I saw nothing but trees and winding road, but no, that wasn't all; there, through the leaves, was a chainlink fence and a cluster of clouds.

"Yeah, I think there actually are—"

"Sheep!" you cried, like a little kid, then proceeded to dash up the road, one hand pressed to your head to keep your beanie from slipping off.

"Ellery!" I sprinted after you, caught up just as you were leaping onto the fence, clinging to it and preparing to climb.

There was a sign on the fence—Private Property: KEEP OUT—and you were blatantly ignoring it.

"Dude, do you see that sign?" I demanded, pointing to it. "You can't go in there!"

You were sitting on the top bar, one leg on each side, a foot in safety and a foot out, and you turned to give me a look of utter exasperation.

"Dude," you teased, "of course I see it. I just don't care."

I tried to call you back again, but the cry died in my throat as you threw yourself over, sailing through six feet of freefall before landing lithely on bent knees. You turned to me and blew a kiss over your shoulder, then took off through the frosty grass and into a herd of very confused sheep.

I sighed, but allowed myself a private smile as I hopped the fence after you.

When I caught up to you, you were standing in front of a sheep, hands on your knees, talking to it as it ate the shrubbery.

"Look at that," you said, pointing at a cloud in the surprisingly blue sky. "Look, it's you!"

I sidled over, hands in my pockets and eyebrows raised. "Ellery Eshelman," I stated in wonder, "you are ridiculous."

You turned to me, beaming mischievously, and let out a glimmering laugh. "I try."

"Yeah, I can see that." I rolled my eyes. "But hey, how about you try somewhere else? We should really get out of here."

"Why?"

I frowned. "Why? Well, because the sign says—"

"Screw the sign, I'm staying right here," you interrupted, then waltzed over and put your hand on my arm. "Sam, in The Hunger Games, did Katniss and Gale let a stupid sign stop them from sneaking out of their district to hunt for food?"

"Well, no, but—"

"So why should it stop us?"

"Well, for one thing, this is real life, and—"

"Screw real life, too!" You shook your head. "Why can't we just pretend like we don't exist?"

"I don't understand," I mumbled.

"Let's be fictional," you implored. "Let's do something that characters in books would do. Let's break the rules and be ridiculous and wreak havoc." A dreamy sigh. "Doesn't that sound fantastic?"

I shifted from foot to foot. I had the feeling that you could make feeding yourself to a hungry lion sound fantastic, if you wanted to. You had too much charisma for your own good. Or mine, I guess.

Anyway, you won.

"All right, Ellery," I conceded. I could feel a fluttering in my stomach, those ever-present nerves, but beside them was that unmistakable hunger for adventure; the wrong-yet-right taste of rebellion. "What is it that fictional people do?"

"Hm," you mused, "let's see." You began a list on your fingers. "For one, they pet sheep. They race also through fields and play hide in seek in forests. Oh, and they roll down hills, regardless of whether there's still melted snow in the grass." With coy eyes, you smirked. "Think you're ready?"

My Polaroid camera was in my pocket, and I could capture everything. I nodded; I was ready. Hopefully.

"Then forgot tonight; forever's gonna start right now." Your words were on fire as you grabbed my hand, a grin alighting your features.

"Come on, Sam," you said. "Let's pretend we don't exist."

Chapter 30

I think you really start to know a person, to understand them, when you people-watch with them; when you sit with them on a bus stop bench in the rain and quietly observe the world as it blurs past; when they are the only thing to stop you from drowning in a sea of muted colors and spinning sound.

I like to think that I knew you before that gloomy Sunday, but I think that was the day that you actually began to make sense, that the contents of your mind were willingly spilled into my hands. At the very least, it helped to pry my eyes open just a little bit further in regards to who you really were.

It was sprinkling outside, but the awning over the bench kept us dry. People hurried by all around, umbrellas unfurled, and took no notice of the girl and boy sitting there and watching them all.

"Look at that guy over there," I remarked, flicking a finger across the street. You looked up, narrowed your eyes—blinked twice as you caught sight of the young man, dressed entirely in firetruck red and standing on a skateboard with a boombox balanced on his shoulder. As the light changed, he glided across the street, taking no notice as he coasted through a puddle and sprayed an army of sensible-shoe tourists.

"Oh my," you said, as he disappeared down the block. That was all, but then there was the flurry of wind-stricken pages, the scratch of ballpoint against the notebook in your lap.

"We'll call him Eric," you told me.

This was how you watched people; you stood aside and let them pass, but froze them momentarily with your pen, captured them in the span of a heartbeat with words on paper. It was, you explained, the way you developed all your characters.

I watched too, helping where I could, but for a lot of the time I studied you out of the corner of my eye. I watched your hair, waves of russet brushstrokes in the air. Your cheeks pink with the cold, your green eyes bright and ringed with makeup. Your lips, candy apple red, pursed in concentration. You were bright and colorful, a peony painted onto the gray afternoon. You were dazzling.

Our tea, to go, sat in paper cups beside us, losing steam with every heartbeat. Occasionally you'd pause, take a sip, and leave a smile for me. Then you'd turn, back to being a silent watcher.

"Look there," you'd say every now and then, pointing to that little girl in pink high heels chasing after her mother, or that tall man with the umbrella who ran into a streetlamp while looking down at his phone. There are characters everywhere, you told me. Just waiting, waiting for someone to find them.

You were bright-eyed when you finally took a break, your scarlet lips knit into a smile. I pulled my camera from my pocket and snapped your picture as you briefly closed your eyes. I was getting a lot of use out of the thing, it's just that nearly every photograph I took was of you.

I watched the captured moment slip out of the camera, and fingered the glossy paper for a moment before sliding it into the notebook with all the others. It was the notebook you'd given me, my Christmas gift, and I'd taken to carrying it everywhere, so that I'd always have a story at my fingertips and because it reminded me so much of you.

You yawned softly, then sighed, your loose bun teetering atop your head. Then you leaned over and kissed me, for no reason except because you could, and wanted to, and no one was going to stop you.

I certainly wasn't, anyway.

When you pulled away, you glanced skyward, where the rain was letting up but the clouds were still looming. A slight frown spiraled your lips, and you adjusted your scarf.

"Autumn leaves are perplexing, Sam," you stated abruptly.

I looked at you; you were concentrating on a tree branch above our heads, bare except for three clinging leaves. Two in gauzy yellow, one in red carpet crimson.

"How so?" I questioned.

You breathed, prepared, gathered words to your chest. "Because they're so—so determined." Your sentence lifted at the end, a question to yourself. Was that what you wanted to say? No—you shook your head.

"That's not the right word," you amended, "but I don't know how else to describe it. I'm just fascinated by the way they cling on like that, through the snow and rain and wind, even though it's not their season anymore and they could just give up."

You paused and thought for a moment. I tried to think of a response, but you spared me the trouble.

"They're like people, I think."

I raised an eyebrow. "How do you figure that?"

"Because...because think about it, Sam. Some of them are quitters; they fall off right away, just give up and let go without even trying. But then others hang on for dear life and refuse to let anything tear them down. Some of them are fighters." You tipped your head back. "Except that their fight is hopeless, either way. They can try all they want, but they can't prevent their evanescent nature, the fact that they're going to burn out in the long run. They won't last forever.

"But I guess," you said, "that's why they're beautiful. We appreciate them because they're only here for a little while." A sigh escaped your lips. "I just wish we could appreciate our lives that way. We're only blinks, just like the leaves, but we take it for granted because our eternity feels longer."

You brushed a wayward strand of hair out of your face, skirting your gaze above my head. Silence fell, and as we watched, a particularly audacious gasp of wind plucked the red leaf from its perch and dragged it into the sky. It turned somersaults in the air and spun against the cloud cover before speeding away down the street.

We leaned over to watch its journey, following it with our eyes as it twisted out of reach of a child's grabbing hands, tickled the tips of a tall woman's hair, slapped against a windshield, but somehow managed to dance away from the wipers in time to catch another gust. It was a splash of candy apple red against a perpetual monochrome, and we watched it until it surfed out of our sights.

We reached for each other's hands. Breathless.

When you looked at me, your eyes were wide like you'd just seen something fantastic, like you'd just had the experience of a lifetime and you were forever changed. It was this expression of realization and self-certainty, and I didn't know how you could get that from a leaf but I didn't doubt that whatever words you were about to say would be glowing.

"Ellery?" I prompted.

It took a moment. You were speaking in lyrics; you were sculpting me a poem right before my eyes. These were your words, your thoughts; your voice was your weapon and the air was your canvas. To get it right, it took a moment of consideration.

"I want to be that leaf," you said at last. "I want to be strong, and a fighter. But...I don't want to hang on forever. I want to know when to let go, and to treat it as an adventure, so I can go out with a bang, like a hurricane or a thunderstorm or—" You sipped the air. "I want to be unstoppable and unforgettable and incomparable and so many other things, countless things, and I don't know how I'm going to manage it all when I have so little time, Sam, I really don't. But I just—I just want to do something. I love watching, but I don't want to sit on the sidelines forever. I want to be in the pictures for once, instead of looking at them. I want to be somebody's everything."

But you are in the pictures, I wanted to say. Here, let me show you, all these pictures of you I have tucked away.

"You are," I said, simple. "You are."

I didn't elaborate; you didn't ask me to. I don't even know if you heard me. Your eyes were fierce and steely and shimmering, and you were looking after the memory of the leaf with bursting intensity. This was yet another side of you, another simplified personality among hundreds. Thousands, maybe.

You are, I repeated, this time in my head. You are, and I couldn't say the rest out loud. You are somebody's everything. You're my everything. And I can only hope that I'm enough.

Epilogue

"The end," I finish, a whisper of scratchy voice on air.

"The end," you echo.

We sit, weightless, on withheld breath and neatly suppressed yawns. The wordless teashop chatter floats around us, competing with the sharp voices on the temporary television screen on the wall. It's dim in here, but darker outside.

I look up. Ten minutes to midnight.

You glance at me, your head against my shoulder, your eyes wide. Smiling, just slightly, I brush your hair behind your ear.

There isn't much to say now. Now that I've emptied my mind, spilled the entire contents of this month into the air. Now that it's just another one of the countless stories told in this listening teashop, words to hide in display mugs and paint themselves onto the walls.

But somehow, saying it out loud makes it feel more concrete, more solid, a tangible thing that really did happen. All fleeting worries of this being a dream are gone now, because you're here in my arms and nothing's ever felt more real.

You're wearing that terrible raincoat again, the bright yellow one that you say your mother got you so you'd always be visible in the snow. It's fitting, I think, that you end the month in the same coat you started, and in the same place, too.

We're really not supposed to be here, I guess. Your parents are throwing a New Year's eve party with extended invites to me and my family, and we were there up until an hour ago. But around eleven, you asked if I wanted to leave, because I'd mentioned that Krystal was having a little get-together at the shop with free tea.

"Greg used to be the life of New Year's," you told me on the way, missing your little brother. "It's not really the same without him."

So I didn't question you, because sometimes you just need something new to wish the old things away. We sneaked out the back and ran through the streets, hand in hand through the air of electric anticipation, and ended up here, soaked by the ever-pouring rain. It's quieter in the teashop, calmer, and I only have to be back in time to drive my presumably drunk aunt and uncle home.

We're still silent. I guess that's all we can be, really, after every-thing I said. We're marinating in the emotions and events, remem-bering them in perfect clarity and storing them away in our minds.

"Tell me a story," you'd whispered in my ear. So I did. I told you our story, which you probably weren't expecting but I didn't care, because I wanted you to know everything. How I'd felt, how I'd always felt; I wanted to see my thoughts as clearly as I was beginning to see yours, even though it probably wasn't necessary. You writers can read people like they're books.

"Five minutes," Krystal calls, her loud voice slicing air as she steps into the main room with a tea tray in her hands. It's packed in here, with people at the tables and on the tables and even littering the carpet. We were lucky to snag that fateful loveseat, although I guess people just don't want to sit on something that has a pretty good chance of falling apart. That's okay, it can just be ours.

"Hi, Krystal," you say as she passes and gives us each a new mug. It's a special tea, something she's reserved for New Year's only.

She pauses. "Hello, Ellery! And Sam, long time no see. Look at you two lovebirds, so cute."

Idle chatter: laughs and blushes and simple questions before she moves on with a smile. Soft voices everywhere, Ryan Seacrest on the screen. Three minutes to midnight.

"A hundred and eighty more seconds, Sam," you murmur, squeezing my hand. Only you would say something like that. Only you could make me smile at it.

We stare at the ball, a glittering sphere in Time Square, waiting to begin its descent. Even though we're seeing this all in playback, I can still feel the bated breath of the crowd.

"I've always wanted to go to Time Square," you say, staring up at the screen and snuggling closer. "At least once in my life, anyway. I want to write about it."

"We will, someday," I tell you.

We. The word slips out so easily now, so effortlessly. Not you, not me, we. Us. I've come to think of us as together always, even though everything is uncertain and the likelihood of forever is devastatingly low. But let's pretend, why don't we? Everything could end tomorrow, but for tonight, today, let's be leaves and cling to our branches. Let's forget we exist for a few breathless heartbeats. Let's lose ourselves in music and drink tea and swallow words and plant both our feet firmly into the moment.

"I hope we will," you whisper.

One minute midnight, and you sigh, take my hands, lift your head to catch my eyes. You say, "This hasn't been a good year for me, Sam. Not by a long shot. But it's been a good month, an amazing month, now that I've met you. So...I don't know what happens next, but thank you. For everything."

Your eyes glisten. I echo it back to you.

"Thank you."

Thirty seconds to midnight, and I look at you. At your green eyes, chestnut hair, button nose, arching smile. And beyond your beautiful face, to your charisma and dauntless soul. The month as I've just told it to you speeds across my mind in fast forward: the first day I saw you, your dance performance, your tears in my living room, Christmas, our first real date. Yesterday. Today. A blank tomorrow.

We've loved and lost, the two of us. We've left. We've led tumultuous lives, but somehow we've found each other in this chaotic crush, joined hands across a chasm. I've done one thing good this year, if nothing else: I've met you.

And with fifteen seconds before this year deserts us, I think of something that I've been thinking about for a while. Something that I've wanted to say for days, but haven't been certain of. I want to mean it; I want it to mean something. I'm hopelessly afraid, but I think I'll always be, and all I can really do is face it.

No excuses, I think, just like back when merely talking to you was the unbeatable hurdle. This is ten stories higher and eight walls thicker, but you've shown me that I can clear it in a single leap.

"Ten," the room chants, gazes on the falling ball.

"Nine." You smile into my eyes.

"Eight." I'm balancing on the precipice.

"Seven." Jump, Sam.

"Six." Three words.

"Five." I look at you, your lips moving as you chant the words. My lips are moving too, but there's a word on them that's too heavy for either of us to fathom, and I'm going to say it. I'm going to say it in:

Three.

Two.

One.

"I love you, Ellery," I say, out loud, for the first time, and it's real and fragile but it feels right as the clock strikes twelve. Your eyes widen, your lips parting, but you don't get to respond because I kiss you, in the middle of the teashop, bright and fearless beneath a chattering chorus of Happy New Year. Your lips are soft and there are fireworks in our minds, fireworks on the screen, powder keg explosions that send us up in flames.

When we pull away, breathless, it's tomorrow. It's next month. It's next year. There are 365 days of blank perhaps waiting for us—but there is also right now. And right now, in this pregnant pause, you're turning to me with a trembling mouth and eyes full of teary wonder.

And then you're saying it—you're saying the words.

"I love you too, Sam."

Then you burst into tears, happy tears, because even though I don't understand it I guess girls are supposed to cry at moments like these. You throw your arms around me, and we're just another kissing couple ringing in the new year amidst all the chatter, yet we're more than that. To us, we're everything, we're anything. We've found each other somehow, and we're not letting go.

"Happy New Year," I murmur, our noses touching.

"Happy New Year," you reply, our breaths synonymous.

I said the end, Elle, but I didn't mean it. I don't want us to end, today or tomorrow or ever, because I can't imagine me without you, because you're a matching puzzle piece in my arms. I know I can't make us last forever, but that doesn't mean I can't try. Let's hold hands and leap into tomorrow, soar on autumn leaf wings. Let's last until we can, then go out with a bang.

I said the end, but let's not call it the end. Because I love you and you love me and I don't know if that's enough but I guess it'll have to be, for us. For now. December is over, but we're not. Let's not end, not ever.

Let's call this the beginning.

9 781930 112858